Before the Dawn

EMMA LESLIE CHURCH HISTORY SERIES

Glaucia the Greek Slave
A Tale of Athens in the First Century

The Captives
Or, Escape From the Druid Council

Out of the Mouth of the Lion
Or, The Church in the Catacombs

Sowing Beside All Waters
A Tale of the World in the Church

From Bondage to Freedom
A Tale of the Times of Mohammed

The Martyr's Victory
A Story of Danish England

Gytha's Message
A Tale of Saxon England

Leofwine the Monk
Or, The Curse of the Ericsons
A Story of a Saxon Family

Elfreda the Saxon
Or, The Orphan of Jerusalem
A Sequel to Leofwine

Dearer Than Life
A Story of the Times of Wycliffe

Before the Dawn
A Tale of Wycliffe and Huss

Faithful, But Not Famous
A Tale of the French Reformation

They dragged him into the monastery gates.

Page 164

EMMA LESLIE CHURCH HISTORY SERIES

Before the Dawn

A Tale of Wyciffe and Huss

BY

EMMA LESLIE

Illustrated by
NORMAN RULT, J. D. WATSON & EDWARD WHYMPER

Constance, Germany

Salem Ridge Press
Emmaus, Pennsylvania

Originally Published
1880
The Religious Tract Society

Republished 2009
Salem Ridge Press LLC
4263 Salem Drive
Emmaus, Pennsylvania 18049

www.salemridgepress.com

Hardcover ISBN: 978-1-934671-27-6
Softcover ISBN: 978-1-934671-28-3

PUBLISHER'S NOTE

At the time in which *Before the Dawn* is set, many believed that the Church could be reformed by a council of the Church leaders. Even after the death of Wycliffe, with Huss being persecuted by the Church, many remained hopeful of a speedy reformation from within. Then, with the shameful matrydom of Huss at the hands of the Council of Constance, these hopes died and instead there came a misguided attempt to usher in reformation through the sword. While human means were failing, however, God was at work. With the great improvement of the printing press came the ability for the widespread distribution of God's Word, while the fall of Constantinople to the Muslims brought to the rest of Europe, scholars that could aid in the further translation of the Scriptures.

Like Conrad, we may be discouraged as we look at the world around us but we must remember the words of Hebrews 4:12, "*The word of God is quick, and powerful, and sharper than any twoedged sword...*" It was through God's Word that the Reformation came at last, and through His Word our lives, our families, and our nation can be reformed again!

Daniel Mills

August, 2009

PREFACE TO THE 1880 EDITION

In the following pages, an attempt is made to delineate the mixture of political and religious feeling that characterized the struggles for religious freedom in England and on the continent of Europe, at the end of the fourteenth and the beginning of the fifteenth centuries. The story illustrated the efforts of the church to purify herself of the corruptions that were a scandal and reproach, and yet to crush out the dangerous heretical tendencies that were everywhere cropping up—the struggles of church and state to maintain their hold upon the peoples of Europe, and keep them still in the blindness of ignorance, in which they had long been content to sleep—with the rising forces that were destined to overwhelm the forms of despotism that had maintained their sway for many generations.

For ages the Church had been asleep—sinking deeper and deeper into lethargy concerning her work in the world, and into the quicksands of luxury and vice. Once she had been the helper of the helpless, the protector of the poor against their oppressors; but now she had forgotten her high mission, and joined hands with the oppressor. Kings and emperors did the bidding of the Church, that the Church might help them to crush the struggles of the people for liberty; while to strengthen herself the Church was glad to make any alliance, be it ever so despicable, or to promote wars and tumults, that the thoughts of men might be turned away from that which intimately concerned each one of them—how they should come to the knowledge of God and the salvation He has provided in Jesus Christ from all men.

If from the dry bones of history I have been able to present to my readers any living picture from which lessons of courage and faith and hope and love may be drawn, and by the help of God's Holy Spirit blossom again in their lives, then the prayers and hopes of the author will be fulfilled, and reader and author may rejoice together in thanksgiving to God for His most precious gifts.

Emma Leslie

HISTORICAL NOTES

A number of important historical figures from the fourteenth and fifteenth centuries are mentioned in *Before the Dawn*. Here is a brief summary of some of these people:

Richard II: Crowned King of England in A.D. 1377, Richard was extremely extravagant, spending enormous sums of money on his luxurious lifestyle without regard for the cost to the English people. Richard was deposed by his cousin, Henry Bolingbroke (who became King Henry IV), in A.D. 1399, and died shortly thereafter.

Wat the Tyler: In A.D. 1381, Wat the Tyler, a blacksmith, became the leader of a revolt against the nobility. The main cause of the revolt was the imposition of a new tax to finance the continual wars with France. After leading the rebels in the destruction of several palaces, Wat the Tyler met personally with Richard II to negotiate peace but was murdered at this meeting. Following his death, the revolt collapsed.

Anne of Bohemia: In A.D. 1382, Richard II married Anne, the daughter of Holy Roman Emperor Charles IV, and sister to both King Wenceslaus of Bohemia and future Holy Roman Emperor Sigismund. Anne successfully pled with Richard to pardon many of those arrested during the peasant's revolt, earning her the title of Good Queen Anne. She died in A.D. 1394.

Geoffrey Chaucer: Chaucer was a well-known poet during the late fourteenth century and also served in various government posts under Richard II. In A.D. 1374, he was appointed Comptroller of Customs for the port of London. It was during this time that Chaucer is believed to have begun his most famous work, *Canterbury Tales.* In this story, he describes a fictional party of pilgrims who take turns telling tales as they travel from London to the shrine of St. Thomas à Becket in Canterbury.

Sir John Oldcastle: John Oldcastle served as a trusted soldier in several military campaigns under King Henry IV. He was also a strong supporter of John Wycliffe and distributed many copies of Wycliffe's writings. In A.D. 1413, Oldcastle was called to stand trial as an heretic. During this trial Oldcastle refused to renounce his beliefs and was quickly convicted and imprisoned in the Tower of London. With the help of a friend, he escaped but four years later he was recaptured and hung and then his body was burned.

Conrad Strickna: One of the early reformers in Bohemia, Strickna was a popular priest who took to preaching in the marketplace when his church could no longer contain the crowds who came to hear him.

HISTORICAL NOTES

Matthias Janovius: Janovius was another early reformer in Bohemia. He was confessor to Emperor Charles IV as well as a writer.

Jerome of Prague: Born in Prague, the capital of Bohemia, Jerome was a close friend of John Huss. After completing his studies at the University of Prague, Jerome traveled widely throughout Europe, including a visit to England where he copied several of Wycliffe's books. In A.D. 1415, Jerome journeyed to Constance where Huss was appearing before the Council. Warned of danger, Jerome fled, only to be arrested a short time later and brought before the Council. He was sentenced to be burned as an heretic and this was carried out the following May.

King Wenceslaus[1] (King Wenzel): Wenceslaus was elected King of Germany in A.D. 1376 and two years later he became King of Bohemia as well. Wenceslaus was a strong defender of John Huss and reform but struggled to maintain his political power. He was deposed on several occasions, including once by his younger brother, Sigismund.

Emperor Sigismund: King of Hungary, King of Germany, and eventually Holy Roman Emperor, Sigismund called the **Council of Constance** in an effort to resolve the disputes between three rival popes. He also personally guaranteed the safety of John Huss at the Council, a promise that, in the end, he was unable or unwilling to fulfill.

[1] Not to be confused with "Good King Wenceslaus" of the Christmas carol, a Bohemian Duke in the 900's.

HISTORICAL NOTES

Pope John XXIII: One of the three rival popes at the time of the Council of Constance, Baldassarre Cossa was an influential Italian cardinal towards the beginning of the fifteenth century. He joined with several other cardinals to call for the **Council of Pisa** in A.D. 1409. In A.D. 1410, following the death of Pope Alexander II, Cossa was elected Pope, taking the name John XXIII. Then, when Emperor Sigismund called the Council of Constance, John was summoned to appear before the Council. He was convicted of crimes against the Church and deposed.

Following the martyrdom of Huss and the death of Wenceslaus, war broke out between the followers of Huss in Bohemia, and the Holy Roman Empire led by Emperor Sigismund. The **Hussite Wars**, as they were called, lasted from 1419 - 1436, and ended with Sigismund being declared King of Bohemia.

The order of the **Black Friars** was founded in the early thirteenth century by Dominic de Guzman to combat heresy within the Church. Their name came from the black cloaks that they wore. Today they are more commonly known as the Dominican Friars.

IMPORTANT DATES

A.D.

1382	Richard II marries Anne of Bohemia
	The Earthquake Council condemns the doctrines of Wycliffe
1384	Death of John Wycliffe
1400	Death of Richard II
1409	The Council of Pisa
1414	The Council of Constance begins
1415	John Huss martyred
1417	Sir John Oldcastle martyred
1418	The Council of Constance ends
1419	The Hussite Wars begin
1431	The Council of Basle begins
1436	The Hussite Wars end
1439	Gutenberg completes his printing press
1453	Constantinople sacked by the Turks

England in the 15th Century

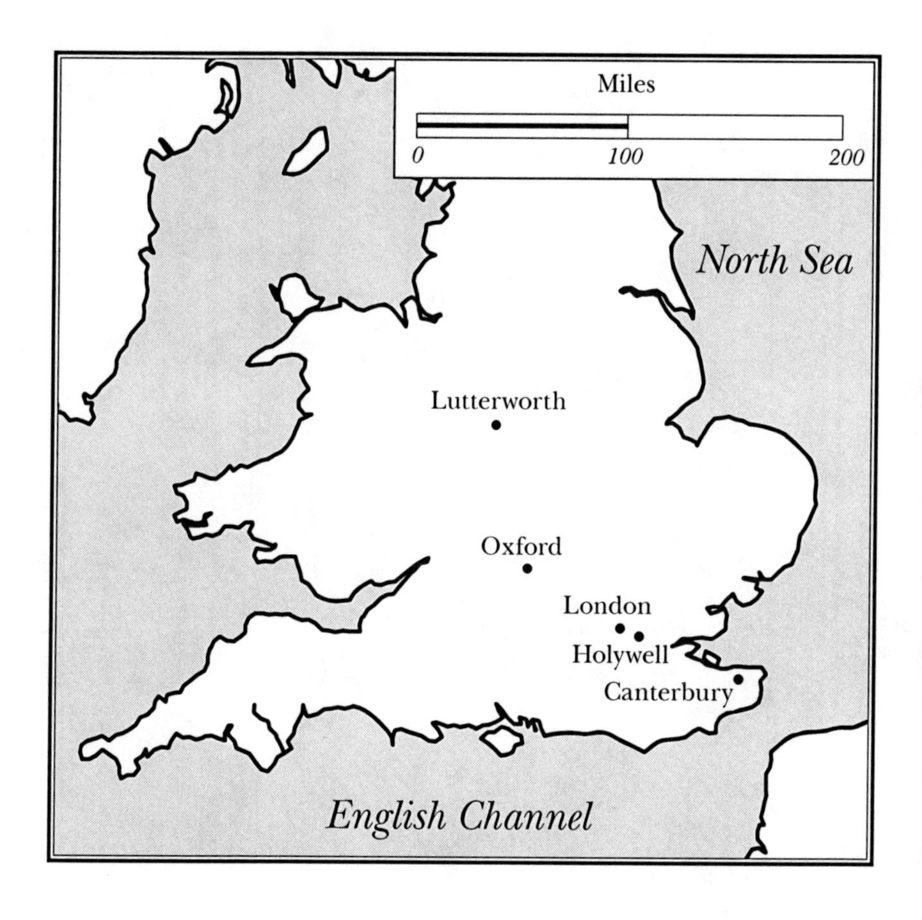

Europe in the 15th Century

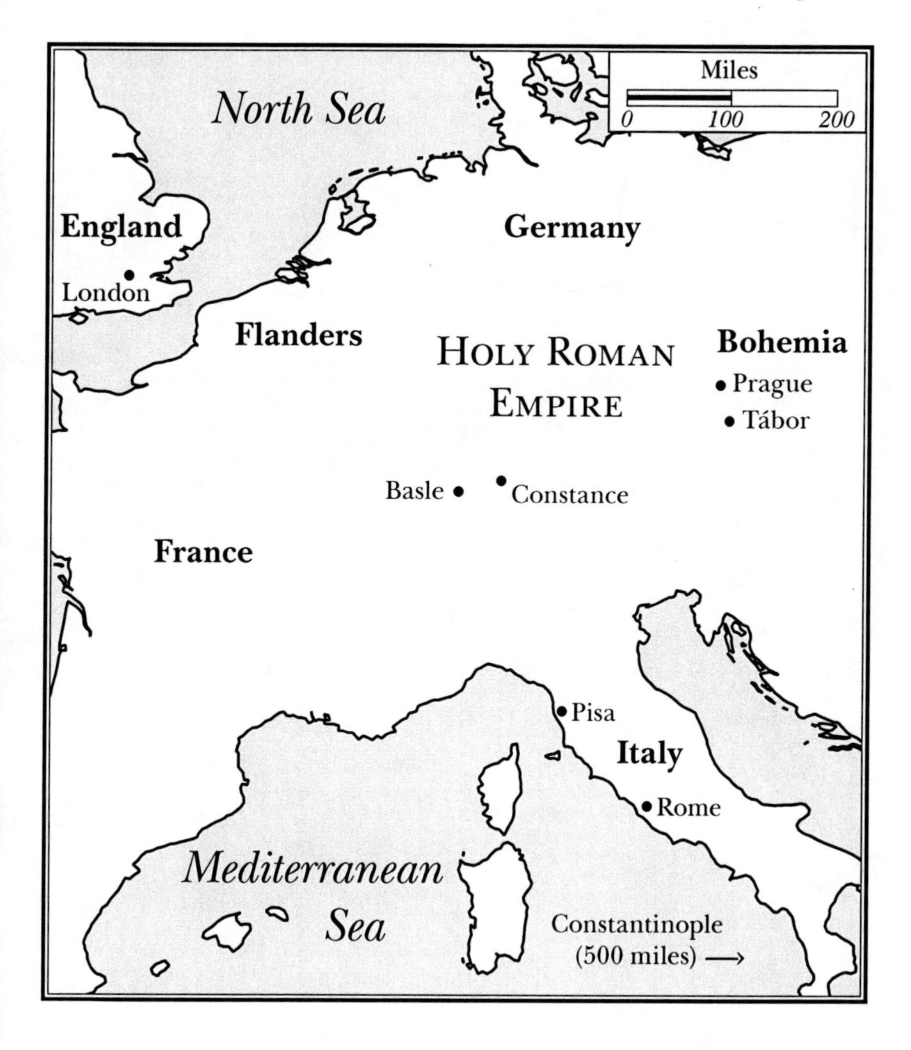

CONTENTS

Chapter		Page

ILLUSTRATIONS

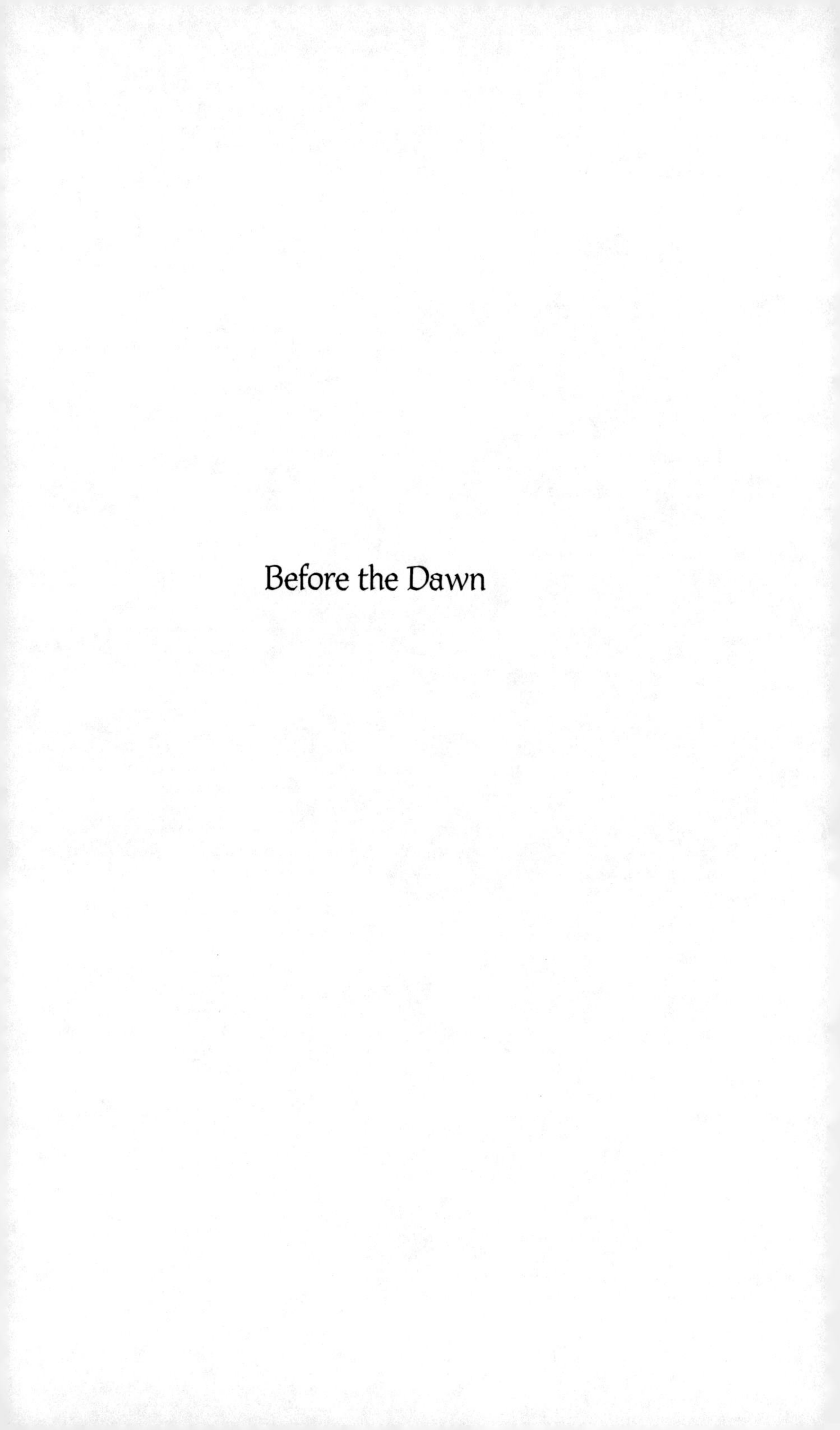

Before the Dawn

Before the Dawn

Chapter I

A Royal Wedding

IT was a gay and animated scene upon which the sun looked down one bright cold day in January, 1382; and the little village of Charing, not far from the royal palace of Westminster, was crowded with a merry throng. They came through the fields of Holborn, or along the road by the river, all bent on the same errand—to see the wondrous plays and magnificent pageants, and join in the festivities that everyone was welcome to partake of on this, the wedding day of King Richard the Second.

Of course, the main topic of conversation was the bride—her beauty, accomplishments, and piety; and, foreigner though she was, and deeply as all foreigners were hated by the English as a nation, it seemed that she had already won for herself a place in the hearts of her people.

GAY: *light-hearted*
PIETY: *devotion to God*

"This is a bright day for England, neighbor!" exclaimed an old man in a leather jerkin, whose brown hands proclaimed his work in the smithy.

His companion grunted, "It might have been, if brave Wat the Tyler had gained for us all he asked; but look ye, it is not for naught the conduits and fountains have been filled with wine and ale again and again by King Richard. But Englishmen will not always submit to be amused like children and slaves; they are beginning to think for themselves, and to feel that the chains gall, and—"

"Faith, neighbor, cease thy grumbling, for this day at least, when our good lord the king would have all men merry as himself," interrupted his friend.

"Ha, merry, forsooth! He would have us drink of his wine because he knoweth that when the wine is in, the wit leaketh out, and he would fain keep us a nation of witless villeins, who dare not ask wherefore new taxes are imposed, or why the king should fix every man's wage."

"Nay, thou hast no cause to grumble at thy wages; thou hast thy full fourpence a day, like any master mason or carpenter; wherefore then, dost thou complain?"

"Because I would fain buy or rent a small plot of land, even as I would have been a yeoman, could I have tilled the soil and tended mine oxen without doing body-service for it to the lord of the land."

"Then 'tis the body-service, and not the wages,

JERKIN: *short, sleeveless jacket*
GALL: *cause great irritation*
FAIN: *rather*

thou art complaining of? Troth, I am somewhat of thy opinion in that matter."

"If thou art any better than the hammer that thou wieldest thou must be of the same opinion; for are we not all of us in slavery? The men of the towns, doubtless, have more privileges than the villeins; but they cannot buy or sell at any fair or mart they please, and our wives may not wear an inch of Flemish broadcloth, and—"

"Nay, if thou art going to bring women and their whimsies about cloth into thy quarrel with the king, thou wilt never come to an end of thy complainings. We must be patient, neighbor; and I say again, this is a bright day for England."

"When she is still a nation of slaves, and brave Wat lies in a dishonored grave?"

"I was not speaking of the sorry insurrection of last year, or even of the king, but of our good Queen Anne. 'Tis of her all men are talking, and many have cause to talk, too; for 'tis to her that many owe their lives, and that they are abroad this day instead of pining within prison walls. Didst thou not hear the story of how she went on her knees before the king to beg for the pardon of all rebels; and the king in his great love could in nowise refuse her request?"

"Ah, but, 'tis said, too, she is no friend to Holy Church, but favoreth these Lollards, like the queen mother and the Duke of Lancaster," rejoined the mason.

VILLEINS: *farmers who owe service to a lord*
YEOMAN: *free farmer*
INSURRECTION: *revolt*

"Well, I have naught to say against the Lollards, they are a peaceable people, honest and—"

"Peaceable!" exclaimed the other, "when they rail against Holy Church, and say that men should read the Scriptures for themselves, and judge what is done by the Church!"

"And wherefore should we not judge for ourselves in the matter of religion, as in other things?" asked a man in a bright pink tabard and a broad white collar.

The mason stared, wondering whether he was the herald or pursuivant of some great lord, who would report all he had heard to his master; but he soon saw that the man wore no armor beneath the short gay tunic, neither was it embroidered with coat of arms or ensign of any sort, and so the gossips breathed more freely.

After a few minutes' silence the man repeated his question, and this time in a louder tone, as though he wished all the crowd to hear it: "Wherefore, I say, should not a man judge for himself in matters of religion? Are we not as able to do this as an idle, ignorant priest, or a lazy, begging friar? We would not heed them in matters of business or daily work, and what know they more than we—at least, more than we can learn if we will?"

Many in the crowd looked shocked, while not a few applauded the bold speech; but a nun who stood near, eager as any to see the fun, and

TABARD: *tunic*
PURSUIVANT: *assistant herald*
GOSSIPS: *close friends*
SERGE: *a heavy fabric*

displaying a bright ribbon of gold tissue over her black serge dress, turned her angry face toward the man, and said, "Thou art overbold to teach thy Lollardism to this crowd; but the Church will crush the evil heresy even yet." And then she turned away from his contaminating presence, while a general move in the crowd, and a loud shout from those in front, attracted everybody's attention to what was going on.

"The fountains are pouring forth right goodly drinks!" exclaimed one.

"Ha, ha! here is wine and ale for all comers; every man can be his own drawer, and none say him nay!" shouted another voice in the crowd.

Of course, everyone was eager to press forward to the fountains just set flowing with strong ale and wine, and there was a good deal of pushing and screaming; but on the whole the crowd was very good-tempered, and as they drew nearer the palace gates there were other attractions provided besides the wine and ale fountains. There were minstrels and mummeries and mountebanks, besides a grand tournament; and in the fields of the nunnery close by there were mystery plays, and games of various kinds going on, in which all were welcome to join.

It was a merry, motley throng that was gathered round the scattered buildings of the convent and the church close by, where a "glutton mass" had

MUMMERIES: *masked frolickers*
MOUNTEBANKS: *sellers of quack medicines*
MYSTERY PLAYS: *religious plays*
GLUTTON MASS: *church feast*

been provided for the refection of the hungry, while from the branches of the bare, leafless trees that enclosed this rich domain of the Church floated pennons and banners of every color and device.

Beneath the trees walked parties of nuns chatting gaily to some young knight or noble lord, for as yet the rule was not imperative upon nuns to keep within the walls of the convent; and, although this was their home—or, rather, abiding-place, for the sweet, sacred name of "home" is almost desecrated by being applied to such institutions—they still mingled rather freely with the world. Monks, and noble ladies in their new-fashioned high-peaked headdresses, and courtiers in parti-colored dresses and shoes a yard long, all mingled with the crowd, while the gay and glittering trappings of the horses lent an additional splendor to the moving panorama.

Our two old friends, the blacksmith and mason, had been separated for a time, and when they met again the first had taken an old lady under his protection. By her dress it was easy to see that she was a foreigner, and the rough boys and 'prentice lads, bent upon extracting fun from everything that came in their way, had teased the old lady sadly until the blacksmith had interfered on her behalf.

She thanked him in broken English, and said she would go home again, but that her little grandson would be disappointed if she failed to tell him

REFECTION: *refreshment*
PENNONS: *pennants*
PARTI-COLORED: *multi-colored*

all about the shows and pageants when she went back.

"Then thou shalt see them all, good dame, if a stout arm can aid thee," said the blacksmith.

"And our little Conrad shall himself thank thee for thy kindness to an old woman," she replied, as she accepted his proffered help to reach a good position for seeing all that was going on.

"Tut, tut; but wherefore did not thy Conrad come to take care of thee himself?" asked the blacksmith.

The old woman smiled for a moment, but it was quickly followed by a sigh as she said: "Our Conrad is a child; but if he were not he would not be able to come here like other boys, for he is sorely crippled, and cannot even stand upright. He will never learn the use of his feet, I fear!" she added.

"Poor little lad! 'twere well if his journey of life were a short one, an it be with so much suffering. I will come and see him, to help thy memory about this day's gay doings, if it will please the child."

"He will be right pleased to talk to thee. We lodge in the house of one Hugh Ryland, in the lane that goeth toward Holborn Fields, hard by the Temple-house."

"What, the cottage that stands near the gate of my Lord of Lincoln's Inn?"

"Yes, that is Hugh Ryland's cottage; and our Conrad will be right glad to see thee, for thou wilt

PROFFERED: *offered*
HARD BY: *near*

be able to tell him more than I can of the shows and mummeries."

"I know the spot, and will come erelong and—" but his speech was here interrupted by his former companion, the mason, being pushed against his elbow; and the next minute another small party of friends had edged their way to his side.

"Lollards!" whispered the mason, looking keenly at the newcomers.

But the blacksmith did not heed the whisper. "'Tis pleasant to see the face of a friend in a crowd like this," he said, as he welcomed them to the little sheltered nook he had discovered.

"'Tis a brave sight," said one, looking round.

"Ha, and 'tis a brave day for England," said the blacksmith, heartily.

"'Tis true, then, that the new queen will show favor to our reformer, Master John of Wycliffe," said one, in a lower tone.

"All men think so, for 'tis well-known that she is a diligent reader of the Holy Scriptures, and favored some in Bohemia who hold views like Master Wycliffe's."

But cautiously as the blacksmith had spoken, his new acquaintance had heard his words, and she drew away from him as far as possible, while a look of hatred and disgust was darted toward the small party of friends who had been called Lollards. She had only just learned the meaning of that word; but to learn it was to hate it with a more rancorous

ERELONG: *before long*
RANCOROUS: *bitter*

hatred than even the bishops and clergy felt against Wycliffe himself.

"I thought we had left the evil thing behind us—that it was far, far away from this England, and that, coming here, I might save the child from the pestilent heresy of his—" and there the old woman stopped, and, forgetting where she was, she covered her face with her hands, and groaned as if in bodily pain.

"Faith, and art thou ill, good dame?" asked the blacksmith, who had heard the woman moan.

"Nay, nay, 'tis naught; attend to thy friends, and heed not me," said the old woman, half-angrily, and trying to push her way through the crowd to get away from such objectionable company.

"The crowd is too much for thee, I trow, good dame," said one of the men; "I fear thou wilt not be able to reach home just yet."

"I will e'en try," said the woman, shortly; for she was determined to get rid of her present company, though she fell a victim to the 'prentices' persecution in consequence.

But the crowd was too great, and too eager to maintain its present position, to allow her to push her way through, so she was reluctantly compelled to accept the help of the blacksmith's stalwart arm again; and even with him to champion her, it was some time before she could reach a spot where she could, without rudeness, tell him that she no longer needed his help. By that time his kindness had

PESTILENT HERESY: *harmful and false beliefs*
TROW: *think*
STALWART: *strong, sturdy*

so far won upon her that, in spite of the strong suspicion she still entertained of his leaning toward Lollardism, she could not but thank him, and say Conrad would be glad to see him, although she hoped that he would forget her, and all she had told him about her grandson, before the next day.

It was useless for her to think of getting more than a passing glimpse at the shows now that she was left alone; and, wearied with the pushing, squeezing, and all the din of music, shouting, and laughter, she was glad to turn her steps toward the quiet lane where she lived.

Chapter II

The Strangers

IN a small wooden tenement, whose overhanging stories threatened to fall upon the heads of every passenger, the blacksmith carried on his trade of an armorer, while in an adjoining shed the more humble work of a blacksmith was carried on.

Master Filpot was reckoned to be a well-to-do citizen, shrewd and prudent, though rather eccentric; but his friend and gossip, Master Trueman, the mason, was ready to doubt everything but the eccentricity this evening; for he had called in to drink a horn of ale and discuss the last item of news about the Lord Mayor and the improvements he was introducing in the city government, when, to his astonishment, he found him preparing to go out.

"Faith, but thou must be tired of thy life to venture forth at this hour. Why, 'tis near five of the clock, and almost dark! Where art thou going?"

"Not far; but I want to see the little knave whose

TENEMENT: *apartment house*
PASSENGER: *traveler*
ECCENTRIC: *odd*

grandam was with us yesterday," said the blacksmith.

"Nay, but if I mistake not, the dame wants none of thee, for I saw she looked with little favor on thy friends, the Lollards."

"Who told thee they were Lollards, Ned Trueman?" asked the blacksmith, a little confused.

"Who but Lollards would speak of the heretic Wycliffe as a 'reformer'? We know that he hath called the Holy Father 'Antichrist,' and 'the most worldly priest of Rome,' and yet—"

"Nay, but what hath all that to do with the little knave who wants to hear about the brave doings of yesterday?" interrupted the blacksmith.

"Naught but this: that thou wilt be befooled for thy pains at going, for the dame hateth all Lollard ways, I trow."

But the blacksmith still went on with his preparations for going out, and when he was ready and had lighted his lantern, asked his friend to go with him.

The mason shrugged his shoulders, grunted and grumbled, but finally set out toward the palace.

They had to pick their way very carefully, for it was almost dark, and the ill-kept roads were full of ruts and holes, while at every dark corner they peered cautiously round, for fear of thieves springing out upon them.

They reached their destination at last, however, with no worse accident than two or three slight

GRANDAM: *grandmother*
BEFOOLED: *made a fool of*

falls; but when the cottage door was opened, Master Trueman found himself in the company of the same little party of friends whom he had stigmatized as "Lollards" a short time before.

The blacksmith laughed at his evident confusion. "Nay, nay, be not afraid, Master Trueman," he said; "these friends have but met to talk how they might help our worshipful Lord Mayor in his efforts to rule righteously this city, and gain for all men more true liberty."

At the word "liberty" the cloud that had suddenly come over the mason's face as suddenly vanished, and he readily accepted the seat that was offered him; though how men could talk about liberty or anything else without a horn of strong ale at their elbows he was at a loss to know, for as he glanced round the room he saw at once that these men were not drinking.

As soon as his friend was seated the blacksmith turned toward the host. "What of thy lodgers, Hugh Ryland; who are they?" he asked.

"I know little about them, but that they came from Bohemia in the train of the queen. One of the great duke's henchmen brought them hither, for the little knave, Conrad, is weakly, and 'twas thought the fresh air from Holborn Fields would be of more service to him than all the balsams of the leech."

"And his grandam, what of her?"

Before answering, Hugh Ryland shrugged his

STIGMATIZED: *marked with disgrace*
IN THE TRAIN: *as attendants*
LEECH: *physician*

shoulders, and then whispered something in his friend's ear.

The blacksmith looked concerned, and glanced toward Trueman as he said, "Thou must be cautious, Hugh, until we know how things may be."

"The Lord Mayor will protect us," said Hugh; "he is himself—"

But the blacksmith held up his finger warningly. "I will see this little knave now, if thou wilt show me the way," he said; and he groped his way up the narrow winding stairs after Hugh Ryland.

The best rooms in the house had been taken for the old lady and her little charge, and various comforts had been sent since from the palace; but to our nineteenth century notions of comfort the place would still seem bare, dirty, and miserable.

The walls were hung with faded tapestry, and the floor was strewn with rushes; but, in the place of sweet herbs being sprinkled with them, fishbones and remnants of meat and pastry were freely distributed among them, and the last layer having been scattered over many previous ones, the air of the room was close and offensive. There was no fire, although it was bitterly cold, and the little pale face, lying on the wooden bolster of the couch, looked pinched and blue, while the large wistful-looking eyes seemed preternaturally bright and eager, as they turned toward the door as it opened.

The next minute, however, a look of disappointment came over the sweet, pale face, and

BOLSTER: *cushion*
PRETERNATURALLY: *unnaturally*

tears dimmed the blue eyes. "I thought it was my mother," he murmured, as the blacksmith came forward.

The old lady, who was sitting near the boy's couch, rose in stately fashion, but there was no warmth of welcome in her greeting.

"Conrad, this is thy visitor," she said, turning toward the boy, and setting the dim oil lamp on an oak chest near the couch; and then, placing a stool for their visitor, she retired into the shadow at the farther end of the room. The child tried to raise himself on his elbow as he thanked the blacksmith for coming to see them; and Filpot then had time to look at the delicate features, and he wondered more than ever who this child could be. He spoke English very fairly, and told him that he was anxious his grandmother should go and see the games, because she had not been out since their arrival at the cottage, and his mother was afraid she would be ill if she did not go out more.

"Who is your mother?" asked the blacksmith.

The child looked surprised at the question. "Dost thou not know that we are Bohemians, and that my mother has been in the service of the Princess Anne?—no, she is the queen now, my grandam says," corrected the boy.

"Yes, she is the Queen of England now, my little knave," said the blacksmith.

"Yes; but we knew her as the Princess Anne, sister of King Wenceslaus, and my mother has served her ever since she was a little girl. She is not a great lady, like some of the court ladies, or else she would not love a poor little thing like me; but being just a poor—"

"Hush, Conrad!" said a commanding voice out of the dusky shadow.

"But Mother says we are poor, although she is an attendant of the queen," persisted Conrad.

The blacksmith, to turn the conversation, asked the boy how long he had been lame.

"I have never been able to walk yet, but I shall now very soon, my grandam saith; for we have heard today of two ways of being cured, and one is sure to make me well."

"What are they?" asked the blacksmith.

"Why, there is the wonderful spring of Holywell. Many miracles of healing have been performed there, for those who are true and devout followers of Holy Church, my grandam hath heard; and then in this city of London, the prior of the Monastery of Holy Trinity hath given certain cottages hard by Houndsditch for poor bedridden folks, who can do naught but pray; and any going to see them on a Friday, and relieving their necessities, will surely be cured by their prayers."

"And thou art anxious to go to Holywell and Houndsditch, I trow," said the blacksmith.

"Thou, too, dost think I shall be cured!" said the boy, eagerly.

"Nay, I cannot tell. This water hath, of a certain,

PRIOR: *head of the monastery*
RELIEVING THEIR NECESSITIES: *providing for their needs*

some medicament in it, for I have heard of folks being cured by it; but of the other—"

"Then Holy Church hath blessed this spring, and made it a well of healing to her faithful children!" said the old woman, eagerly.

The blacksmith turned toward the shadowy part of the room where Conrad's grandmother still sat.

"Nay, good dame; I said not that the Church had aught to do with it, except in the way of taking toll and tithe of those who drink the water. God Himself hath given it certain healing powers, I doubt not; but whether it can cure lameness, I know not."

"Thou hast never heard of such being cured by it?" asked the boy, a little anxiously.

"'Tis only of sickness and rheums I have heard people have been cured; but still I say not that it cannot cure thee if thou couldst go thither."

"Oh, I will, I must go!" said the boy; and he turned restlessly on his straw-stuffed couch, as if anxious to set off at once. After a few minutes' pause, he said:

"My grandam could go and ask all these folk at Houndsditch to pray for me; my mother would give her silver pennies for each of them. Think you not that their prayers and the holy water together would make me strong like other boys?"

The blacksmith wished he could give the little lad some hope, but he had no faith in the miracles

MEDICAMENT: *medicine*
TOLL AND TITHE: *a fee*
RHEUMS: *runny noses*

that were falsely said to be wrought by this water; and as to the prayers of the feeble folk of the priory, though he would by no means dissuade any from a charitable work, still he doubted not that this was used by the priests to lead men to trust in the prayers of others instead of going themselves to God for what they needed.

He said something of this to little Conrad; but the boy quickly interrupted him. "Thou dost think that because we came from Bohemia we are not faithful children of Holy Church, and therefore God will not help us," he said.

"Nay, nay, my little lad; many of God's faithful servants are in Bohemia, I trow."

"We are true to Holy Church," said the old lady, in a stately tone. "We consort not with those who despise her and speak evil of the pope."

"Well, well, good dame, I have naught to accuse thee of in this matter; if thou dost read the Scriptures thou dost know—"

"The Scriptures!" interrupted the boy; "dost thou mean the Bible?"

"Yes, 'tis indeed God's Word, as doubtless thou knowest."

"My mother did but mention it once—that the Princess Anne spent some hours each day in the study of this book; and she would fain have me learn to read it too."

"When did she say this?" burst forth the old woman, starting from her seat and speaking in an angry tone.

CONSORT: *associate*

"Nay, Grandam, why shouldst thou be angry? If this book be good for the Princess Anne it were surely good for me."

"Good for thee!" almost shrieked the old lady; "it hath cursed thee, and thy father and mother too. The reading of this book, which the Church hath forbidden, will work sore woe to Bohemia and to England, if it be not stopped."

"Nay, nay, good dame; speak not so. Hast thou seen the book for thyself?"

"Ah, many times have I seen it in a hand that is well-nigh wasted away by this time, I trow."

"But hast thou read it for thyself?" asked the blacksmith, quickly.

"Nay; praise the saints and holy virgin! I cannot read—have had naught to do with this evil device of Satan."

"Oh, Grandam, call it not an evil device; for thou knowest that my mother doth greatly desire that I shall learn this clerkly art."

The old lady groaned. "Thy mother will curse thee wholly, in spite of all I may do to save thee. Clerkly art, dost thou call this reading? Our priests and friars are fain to leave the evil thing alone, for few of them can read."

"Ah! to their shame, and not to their praise, be it said that they are both ignorant and idle," said the blacksmith, warmly.

"Nay, nay; speak not evil of the holy friars, to anger my grandam," said little Conrad; "but tell me all thou dost know of this Bible. My mother saith it

CLERKLY ART: *reading*

is a wonderful book; and the queen, her mistress, loveth it right well, as doth also the king's mother and the Duke of Lancaster. Grandam, thou dost not think that the Princess Anne would meddle with aught that is evil?" he added.

"What may be good for queens and dukes may be evil for poor folk like us. The Church, in her wisdom, hath said that the ignorant and unlearned may not read the Bible; and, as a faithful servant of the Church, I must obey, and so must thou, Conrad."

The boy looked puzzled, but not convinced, by what his grandam said. "I should like to see this book for myself," he said. "Canst thou read?" he suddenly asked the blacksmith.

Master Filpot shook his head rather sadly. "I would to God that I could," he said, earnestly.

"Dost thou know anyone who can?" asked Conrad.

"Yes, there are one or two good citizens here in London whom I have heard could read," said Filpot, cautiously.

"Then wherefore dost thou not learn of them?" asked Conrad. "I would that I knew one who could teach me," he added, with a sigh.

The blacksmith sat and mused in silence for a few minutes, and then he whispered, "Wilt thou persuade thy grandam to let thee learn?"

"Oh, never fear, but my grandam will be willing, when she seeth I cannot be content with aught but this. She loveth me right well, good sir, and will not say me nay when she seeth my heart is set upon it."

"Then I will try and learn of those who can teach, and then thou shalt learn of me, if thou canst. It will pass away many a weary hour when thou art lying here on thy couch, and—"

"Nay, nay; but I am not going to lie here much longer. Hast thou forgotten the wondrous Holywell we were talking of and the feeble folk by Houndsditch, whose prayers my grandam will buy for me?"

"And wherefore shouldst thou not pray for thyself?" asked the blacksmith.

Conrad looked astonished and something like a shudder seemed to shake his slight frame. "Pray for myself!" he repeated; "would you have *me* pray to God? Nay, nay! it would—it would be awful!" and the boy covered his face with his hands and shivered with terror. "Don't, don't talk about praying to God again," he said. "I can pray to the saints, and to the sweet mother of mercy, the holy virgin; but oh, not to God! not to God!"

"But God is—"

"Sir, dost thou not see that thou art frightening the child? Thou must perceive, too, that it is useless to try and teach him thy heresy, this Lollardism, for he hateth it as sorely as I do;" and the old lady came forward majestically, and took a seat near the couch.

SAY ME NAY: *tell me no*

The blacksmith rose to leave at once, for he feared that he had already said too much; but in a moment the boy was trying to raise himself again.

"Thou wilt come to see me very soon, to teach me this reading?" he said, eagerly.

"Yes, I will come," said the blacksmith, in spite of the old lady's sour looks.

Chapter III

A Night Encounter

"THAT man is a Lollard!" This was Dame Ursula's exclamation as the blacksmith went downstairs.

Conrad looked at his grandmother, and then at the door by which his visitor had left. He had been taught to hate the name of "heretic" before he left Bohemia, and he knew that "Lollard" was a term of reproach quite as bitter in its meaning, and that Wycliffe, the leader of such, was hated by the pope and clergy, and had been summoned to appear before the bishops in London, and would have been condemned but for the interference of the king's mother and the powerful Duke of Lancaster, who was sometimes called the Father of the Lollards.

All this had been told him by his grandmother, as well as many false stories concerning the evil wrought by these people, so that at the bare mention of the blacksmith being a Lollard he shuddered again with disgust and fear.

"Why dost thou think the man is a Lollard, Grandam?" he asked.

"Because of the way in which he spoke of the Bible. This Wycliffe hath translated it into the English tongue, so that unlearned men may break the laws of Holy Church, and read this book, to the destruction of their souls."

"But, Grandam, if the book be bad, as thou sayest, why doth the Princess Anne read it?"

"By my faith, Conrad, thou wilt anger me if thou sayest aught about the book or the Princess Anne again. I tell thee it is forbidden by the Church, and that is enough to make me hate it, and should be enough for thee, if thou wert not tainted with this hateful heresy!"

Poor Conrad burst into tears at his grandmother's angry words. The idea of being "tainted with this hateful heresy" was worse than all; and he sobbed so violently that it was some time before his grandmother could pacify him.

"Thou wilt not think I am 'tainted with heresy' because I want to learn to read?" he said, when the sobbing had somewhat subsided.

"There, hush, Conrad! thou knowest I can refuse thee nothing; thou shalt learn to read, and this blacksmith shall teach thee; but thou must surely beware of the man, for I do greatly fear he is a Lollard."

If Dame Ursula had gone downstairs just then her suspicions about this would have been confirmed, and she would have known, too, that her landlord, Hugh Ryland, and many of his friends, were "tainted with this heresy." On the appearance of the blacksmith among them once more, the party downstairs ceased their discussion about "liberty" and "taxes," and "land tenure by the payment of money instead of body service," which had so greatly interested Master Trueman; for his friend, taking a rather curious-looking key from under his leather jerkin, where it had been concealed, went into an opposite recess, and after a few moments returned with a clumsy-looking volume, which he handed to one of the company, and then seated himself near his old friend.

Trueman looked from one to the other, greatly puzzled to understand what this might mean, for all the party had settled themselves to listen attentively, while the reader carefully and reverently turned over the coarse leaves of the clumsy book. It was not illuminated with pictures on the margin, like most books written by the monks, who were the only writers of those days; and, seeing this, Trueman began to get fidgety. But at this moment the blacksmith whispered, "'Tis of liberty the book tells, and it was penned by a godly priest of Cornwall, one John Trevisa."

"'Tis not Wycliffe's?" asked Trueman, suspiciously.

"Nay, 'tis written by the priest of Cornwall, and was first done for my lord Berkeley, who hath a great regard for this book."

LAND TENURE: *holding land*
ILLUMINATED: *decorated with gold, silver and bright colors*

The reader had found the place, and now, in a clear, reverent voice, he slowly read the story of the Prodigal Son, everyone listening with earnest attention, and none more impressed than Trueman. When the reading was over prayer was offered, and then a hymn or psalm was sung in a low voice.

This last exercise again startled Trueman.

"This singing, or lulling, is a Lollard practice, by my faith!" he whispered, as it was concluded.

But the blacksmith did not heed his words. He took the precious book and locked it up in its hiding-place once more, again concealing the key beneath his jerkin.

When he had wished the rest of his friends farewell, and he and Trueman were outside in the darkness, he said, "What of the reading, Ned Trueman? Didst thou ever hear such words before?"

"By my faith, I never did. Why, 'tis better than the preaching of the bishop at Paul's Cross; and I have heard him there rating the Lollards most soundly, after the heretic Wycliffe had got off."

"Never mind Wycliffe or the bishop either just now, but tell me, art sorry thou camest with me?"

"Nay, nay; for right sensible men were they that were with Hugh Ryland, although they eschew the good ale which thou knowest I love to quaff when talking."

"Nathless they thought the talk would be better without the ale."

RATING: *rebuking*
ESCHEW: *avoid*
NATHLESS: *nevertheless*

"Well, right goodly talk it was; and if our citizens and hot-headed 'prentice lads would give heed to such counsel as they say our Lord Mayor is ready to give, instead of wasting their time junketing at Finsbury Fields, the liberty we want might be gained, I trow, sooner than by fighting or rioting for it."

"And the reading—was it as good as the talk?" asked Filpot, rubbing his hands with delight.

"Good! 'Twas better than anything I ever heard before; and, Master Filpot, I tell thee this—I am a better judge in such a matter, I trow, than thou art, seeing I am the father of a wayward son, who hath gone into a far country, and thou hast never had wife or child. I tell thee that book is true."

"And wherefore dost thou judge it to be true, Ned Trueman?" asked his friend.

"Because the father in the book going to meet his son, and forgetting all his offenses for joy at his return, is just what every father would do if he had the chance. I would, Master Filpot, if I only knew where my son was. I would journey to the far country myself and fetch him back."

It was the blacksmith's turn to be startled now, for he did not know that his friend had a son; and to hear the usually stern old man speak as he now did was altogether so surprising that for a minute or two he could only walk on in silence, and wonder at what he had heard.

At last he managed to say, "If anybody told thee

JUNKETING: *merrymaking*

that book was false and evil, wouldst thou believe them?"

"I would not believe that what I have heard to-night is false or evil, for I have that within me that tells me it is true and good, if loving one's children be good."

"And thou dost not believe it to be evil!"

"Nay, nay; 'tis the want of love that is the evil, I trow. If I had not been so stern with my boy—but there, 'tis useless to tell thee of that, now that he's gone, only this: I know the father that book tells of is a true father, for I know it here;" and the old man laid his hand on his heart.

At this point the conversation was suddenly interrupted by the two friends being seized from behind and their arms firmly pinioned. The blacksmith feared that spies must have been near Hugh Ryland's cottage at some time, and that they were now seized as suspected Lollards; but Ned Trueman, having no such fear, called most lustily for the watch. "Watch! watch!" resounded again and again; and several windows were opened close by, and the people, hearing that someone was in distress below, took up the cry, so that by the time the ruffians had succeeded in stopping Trueman's mouth a dozen other voices had taken up the cry of "Watch! watch!" while lanterns began to cast a flickering light here and there, and the distant clatter of horses' hoofs and the shouts of the watchmen announced the approach of the night patrol.

PINIONED: *pinned*

The neighborhood being aroused, the footpads thought it would be best to make their escape without delay, which they did with little difficulty in the darkness; and by the time the watch came up Master Filpot and his friend had somewhat recovered from their fright and alarm. But the thieves having escaped, the leader of the watch seemed disposed to treat their victims rather roughly.

"Who are ye, and what called ye abroad at nine of the clock on a winter's night?" he asked, savagely.

Trueman answered with almost equal temper; but the blacksmith, who knew that he had been to a meeting that might involve himself and friend in a good deal of trouble, answered more coolly and warily than his companion.

"And so you would fain have us believe ye are honest citizens; but how comes it, master blacksmith, or armorer—for ye are both, I trow—how comes it then, I say, that ye are so often abroad, when all other honest folks are in their beds?"

Master Filpot almost trembled with anxiety, for to be suspected of a leaning toward Lollardism might be ruin; but Ned Trueman, who was thoroughly roused, answered shortly and sharply, "And are ye honest watchmen and our fellow-citizens, or soldiers of King Richard, that ye would rob us of our liberty and shut us within doors at the setting of the sun? We be honest men; and if our business take us abroad at night as well as day, is it aught to any man but ourselves?"

FOOTPADS: *robbers*

"Then ye may look to yourselves if the rogues fall upon ye again," said the watchman, climbing on his horse with as much speed as his cumbrous armor would permit. "Come, my men," he called to the scattered patrol; and they had scarcely moved on their way before there was another terrified scream of, "Watch! watch!" in the next street.

Our two friends did not go to see how their fellow-victims fared, but hastened home with all speed; where, after seeing that the house was made secure against a midnight attack of another class of thieves, Master Filpot sat down to muse over the events of the evening.

It was not often that he sat down to think as he now did, but the occurrences of the last hour or two made him feel troubled and anxious. First, there was the promise he had given to Conrad about the reading lessons. Now that he came to think about the matter more calmly, he greatly doubted his power to learn this art himself. He was getting on in years, although by no means so old as his friend, Ned Trueman; and then his mind was so occupied with the cares of his business that he greatly feared his memory would fail him if tasked with such unwonted work as remembering the forms of the different letters. Altogether he thought the project must be given up, and he would not go to see Conrad again.

Then he thought of Ned Trueman, and the risk he had incurred by introducing him to their secret

CUMBROUS: *bulky*
UNWONTED: *unusual*

meeting. He had long desired that his old friend should share the privilege he enjoyed of hearing God's Word read, believing that the old man would soon cast off the superstitions of the corrupt Romish Church, and embrace the liberty with which God makes His people free; but now that he had taken the—for him—daring step of introducing him to the little congregation of Lollards that met to read his book, he felt half-afraid of what he had done, and was ready to blame himself as being too rash, in spite of what Ned Trueman had said on their way home.

Then last, but not the least cause of continued alarm, was the attack made upon them on their way home, and the questioning of the watchman as to the business that took them abroad at that hour of the night. All these causes of disquietude by no means tended to raise Master Filpot's spirits, and he went to bed full of anxious care concerning the future, and the trouble he felt sure it had in store for him. Poor man! he forgot he had a Father in heaven who was ready to relieve him of the burden, if he would only cast it upon Him. Perhaps he had never heard the loving command of the apostle, "Casting all your care upon him, for he careth for you."[1] "The word of the Lord was precious in those days;"[2] for although Wycliffe had translated the Scriptures into English, as well as the monk of Cornwall, John Trevisa, still as the art of printing was yet unknown, copies of these

[1] I Peter 5:7 [2] I Samuel 3:1

PRECIOUS: *valuable because it was scarce*

translations could be multiplied only by the slow and tedious process of writing.

He was envied by many for his possession of the Gospels. They had cost him a very splendid suit of armor, and he thought the book a wonderful bargain at that price, for sometimes it took the savings of a lifetime to purchase only one of the Gospels, and he was so rich as to have all four. But while thinking of his treasure as he lay in bed, he suddenly remembered that he had not seen the key of the chest where it was kept since he had been home, and he got up at once to look for it, unfastening all his clothes, for people slept in them in those days. But no! hunt as he would, no key could be found. He searched the floor, and went down into the lower rooms; but he could not find it, and with a groan of fear and apprehension he threw himself on his straw pallet once more, and tried to remember whether he had not felt for it after the thieves had left them.

But no thought of the key had entered his mind until he had gone to bed, and so, try as he would, he could not recall any remembrance of being possessed of it after leaving Hugh Ryland's cottage.

This additional anxiety deprived him almost entirely of sleep for that night, and as soon as it was light he got up to search once more for the key of his treasure. But it seemed hopelessly lost, unless it had been left at Hugh Ryland's; and to ascertain this he resolved to go to the cottage in the course

ASCERTAIN: *make certain of*

of the day and ask if it had been found there. No, Hugh had not seen it; but, hearing of what had happened, he advised that inquiries should be made in the street, for if some of the neighbors had found it they would be willing to restore it.

"Ah! but they will ask what my treasure is, if I tell them I have lost the key of a chest," said the blacksmith, timidly.

"Nay, nay, they will not; and should any question thee about it, tell them it is a work thou prizest; but many would not think it of as much value as the chest in which it is kept. This is true, as thou knowest, Master Filpot, for the Word of God is condemned by many in these days."

"But marry, Hugh, if they—"

"Nay, nay; the Lord our God will provide thee with an answer when the question doth come, and, it may be, will bring good out of this seeming evil," said Hugh, cheerfully.

The poor blacksmith seemed to gather strength and courage from his conversation with Hugh, and he set out to make inquiries with renewed hope of recovering his treasure. True, he might easily have forced the lock, but he was troubled that the key should be in perhaps unfriendly hands. Might not the attack itself have been a scheme to get the cherished volume into the possession of those who would make it a ground of bitter persecution, already threatened from more than one quarter?

MARRY: *an exclamation, used to express amused or surprised agreement*

Chapter IV

Geoffrey Chaucer

To one accustomed only to the quiet of the country, the noise and din existing in the busy streets of the city were almost bewildering. Crowds of people stood round the open stalls—for there were no shops in those days—each chaffering with the merchant to obtain the article he sought to purchase at the lowest possible price, while the 'prentice lads ran hither and thither, helping their masters to exhibit their wares, or shouting at the top of their voices the prices and merits of their goods. Flemish peddlers, selling hats and spectacles, shouted, "Buy, buy! what will ye buy?" while the drapers' assistants seized passengers by the shoulder, and compelled them to look at the velvet, and lawn, and silk, and Paris thread. A little farther on, and the blacksmith's ears were deafened with the cries of, "Hot sheep's feet and mackerel;" then came the stalls where pepper and saffron, spices and green ginger, were thrust before his eyes.

CHAFFERING: *bargaining*
LAWN: *fine linen*

It was in the neighborhood of these grocery stalls that he had been attacked the previous night, and so it was here he must make his inquiries. He began this business by making a purchase. Some pepper and saffron were ordered, and while these were being weighed he spoke about the attempt to rob him, and asked if a key had been found by anyone near there. Everybody had heard of the attempted robbery, but these night attacks upon unwary foot passengers were of such common occurrence that no one thought much of them. The loss of a key was a more serious matter, and the merchant sent one of his 'prentice lads to make inquiries among the other shopkeepers; but he came back in a few minutes, saying he could hear nothing of it.

"If thou wilt step in and speak to the dame, she will, doubtless, ask her wenches, for they may have heard something of it;" and the obliging merchant led the way into his house at the back of the stall. Groping his way through bags of pepper and boxes of spices that seemed to occupy all the lower part of the house, he went upstairs to the family room, where a lady and her two daughters sat busily plying the distaff.

"Here, dame, I have brought thee a gossip who hath lost a key, and would fain have thee ask the wenches whether either of them found it;" and a meaning glance was exchanged between the merchant and his wife.

DISTAFF: *a staff used in spinning wool or flax*

After her husband had left the lady looked keenly at Master Filpot, and then said, "Is the key thine own?"

"Yes, it is the key of a chest that—that—" and then the blacksmith stopped, fearing he should betray his secret.

"And the chest—what doth it contain?" asked the lady.

"Nay, that is my own business, good dame. If thy wenches know aught of this key, bid them restore it, I pray thee, and I will give them a silver penny each."

"We need not the money, good sir; but 'tis my daughter who is anxious that this key shall be given to none but the rightful owner, for she hath had it in her hand aforetime, and knoweth what is in the chest." These last words were said in an impressive whisper, and the lady looked closely at the blacksmith while she spoke.

His newfound courage forsook him in a moment. "Thou dost know what the chest containeth!" he stammered.

"My daughter hath seen it—hath read it," said Dame Winchester, in a whisper.

A ray of hope darted across the blacksmith's mind: "Then ye are—"

"We are friends of the new Lord Mayor. We desire to see many things reformed," said the lady, cautiously.

"But—but my secret is safe?"

"Yes, safe as thy key;" and she pushed aside the

arras, and took it from a little receptacle in the wall.

Master Filpot was so overjoyed at recovering his treasure that he forgot all his fear, and confided to Dame Winchester the secret of their meeting in Hugh's cottage to read the Scriptures.

The lady smiled. "'Tis not so great a secret as thou deemest it," she said.

"But we have not been betrayed, I hope?" said her visitor, in some alarm.

"Nay, but there are more friends of godly Master Wycliffe than meet near Lincoln's Inn. Fear not, for though my daughter hath seen thy book, and read from it one night when thou and Master Goldby were away, she would not betray thee; no, not if King Richard himself commanded it."

Thus reassured, the blacksmith went on to tell of his visit to Conrad and his grandmother, and the child's desire to learn to read. "I have promised to learn myself, that I may teach him," he concluded, with something of a sigh.

"Thou wilt not find it easy work at thy time of life, I trow," said Dame Winchester. "My daughter was long in learning the look of the curious black marks, and yet the wench was anxious to learn, and deft at learning, too."

"I wish she could teach the little knave, and save my old brains."

"She might if she were abiding at home, for 'tis not so far from Chepe to Hugh Ryland's cottage but she might walk thither daily on such an

ARRAS: *tapestries*

errand, especially if the child wants to learn that he may read the Scriptures. But she goeth to her aunt's next week, who liveth near to Holywell, and, therefore—"

The blacksmith interrupted her at this point: "Little Conrad hath taken a craze to go to Holywell, for the child is lame, and hath been told that the waters of the spring will heal him. I will talk to his grandam, and persuade her to take the child thither to live for a time, and then thy daughter—"

Just at this moment the forked beard of the merchant was seen, as he thrust his head from behind the arras that hung in front of the door.

"What is it about the wench?" he asked; and then without waiting for an answer, he said:

"I have brought the worshipful Comptroller of Customs for this our part of London, Master Geoffrey Chaucer, to see thee, dame;" and the merchant bustled about to find the best seat in the room for his visitor.

He was anxious to do him honor, for he stood high in court favor, and, moreover, in his capacity of Comptroller of Customs, might possibly have it in his power to help forward or hinder some of the merchant's business.

But Dame Winchester forgot all about bags of pepper and boxes of saffron when she heard the name of "Master Geoffrey Chaucer," for her daughter Margery had told her a wonderful tale of his

Meeting Master Geoffrey Chaucer

wit and learning and skill in poetry only the day before, and how he had been heard to say that he would pull the cowl from monkish heads, and show the world something of their wickedness; and she wondered now whether he was a favorer of the Lollards, or only hated the priests because he saw through their hypocrisy.

The lady was so overawed with the thought of Master Chaucer's learning that, after curtseying in a stately fashion, she could only sit and stare in silent wonder, while her husband entered upon the business that had brought the comptroller to him, until he suddenly turned to his wife and said, "Master Chaucer will dine with us, dame."

The good-natured merchant knew nothing of household management, and had not the least idea of putting his wife into such a flutter of fear and anxiety as he did. She left the room, leaving the blacksmith in a most uncomfortable position; he seemed to have been forgotten by everybody, for the lady had dismissed her daughters before entering into conversation with the blacksmith, and now, in her anxiety to find them and set them to work, she forgot everything else.

"Margery, Alice, where are ye? Come, come, my wenches, we must hurry to the kitchen and the buttery, for your father hath asked Master Chaucer to dinner."

"Master Chaucer!" exclaimed both girls in a breath.

OVERAWED: *intimidated*
BUTTERY: *pantry*

"Mother, will he tell us anything of his wondrous poesy?" asked Margery.

"He will ask if thou hast ever seen aught besides salt fish and cabbage for dinner if we are not quick," retorted her more practical sister.

"Mother, Master Chaucer hath dined at court; we can never prepare dinner for him," said Margery, in dismay.

"Nay, but we must," said Dame Winchester. "He knoweth the law forbidding citizens to have more than two courses at dinner; and as the crane that was roasted yesterday hath not been cut, I will put it again on the spit, and bid Deb see that it doth not burn."

"There is some stewed porpoise left and a high pasty."

Dame Winchester began to breathe more freely now. Like a general reviewing his forces, she went through her buttery, calculating how many dishes she could send to table on such a short notice. With the help of her daughters, several smaller castles of pastry were soon prepared, and these, with the high one already baked, and a few tigers, lions, and angels of jelly, would be sufficient for the second course; while for the first there were the crane and stewed porpoise, and plenty of parsnips and carrots.

To dress for dinner was as important in those days as in these; but not until every dish was ready to set on the table could Margery or her sister

POESY: *poetry*
CASTLES OF PASTRY: *pastries shaped like castles*

hope to leave the kitchen, for it was their province to prepare the meals, while Deb, their one maid-servant, did the dirty work of the house. The art of cooking was carefully learned by all ladies in those days, and Margery would have been as much ashamed of a broken tiger or an ill-made castle at the table, as we should be of a torn dress or some great breach of etiquette.

And so, while they dressed themselves in their new-fashioned gored kirtles, or skirts, that fitted them almost tight round their ankles, with scarcely a fold, their talk was all about the dishes they had been preparing, and their anxiety lest one of them should prove a failure and bring disgrace upon them.

But the upper table, where Master Winchester and his guest would sit, with their mother and themselves, was by no means a sight to be ashamed of when all the dishes were set on. The roasted crane, decorated with some of its own feathers, and gold and silver leaves, formed a handsome center, while round it were grouped the smaller dishes of vegetables and the stewed porpoise. The dishes themselves were a curiosity in those days, and costly too, and the girls were proud of their new possession; for to have the new-fashioned crockery-ware instead of silver dishes, such as could be hired anywhere in the city, proclaimed their father one of the richest merchants in Chepe. It was not the fashion for even grown-up young ladies to join in

GORED: *made of multiple panels of cloth*
CENTER: *centerpiece*

the conversation of their parents unless invited to do so; and Dame Winchester was too anxious to see her guest well-served—that the gold cup at the side of his plate was duly filled with the famous London ale, or mead—to pay much attention to the talk of her husband and Master Chaucer; but Margery forgot even her manners in the interest of listening, and dipped her fingers at random into her plate, regardless of the laws of etiquette, which forbade more than the tips to be used, or a crumb to be dropped as it was being conveyed to the mouth.

The merchant and his guest discussed all sorts of matters—the late marriage of the king, and the influence Anne was likely to have over him, and how it would be used. From Master Chaucer's position as one of King Richard's esquires, he would probably be able to tell them the truth about court affairs, and Master Winchester wanted to know whether the general belief about the queen was correct.

"That she is a right merciful and gracious lady men are well-assured, from what she hath already done for the witless rebels who followed Wat the Tyler, and lay groaning in prison for their misdeeds; but 'tis also said she is a pious lady, which I take to mean that she will be led by her confessor and the clergy to—to well, to bind England more fast to the feet of the pope."

Master Chaucer smiled. "Thou art no friend of the clergy, I perceive; but fear not the piety of the queen, for she is, doubtless, as much a Lollard as

ESQUIRES: *gentlemen attendants*

thyself." This was said in a lower tone, so that the servant and 'prentices sitting at the lower table below the salt might not hear; but Master Winchester looked alarmed.

"I—I am friendly to the counsels of our Duke of Lancaster," he said.

"And he is well called the father of this Lollardism, for it is through him that Master Wycliffe is preaching at Oxenford still, instead of languishing in some monastery dungeon."

"And thou, Master Geoffrey—what dost thou think of this Lollardism?"

But the comptroller shrugged his shoulders. "I may help it, if I be no Lollard myself," he said, enigmatically.

"Thou wilt help it with thy poesy?" the merchant said, questioningly.

"Ah! men will read poesy, I trow; and the follies and evil lives of the clergy—monks and friars, bishops and priests—shall be made known to all the world. Will it not make men seek other guidance, think you, when they learn that their guides are more blind than themselves?"

"Ah! that will they, and Master Wycliffe's wonderful book of the Scriptures will be more eagerly sought than ever;" and speaking of the Bible brought to his remembrance their slighted visitor, the blacksmith.

"Didst thou forget the poor man I brought to thee this morning, Margery?" he said, suddenly turning to his wife.

BELOW THE SALT: *salt was only available at the head table*
ENIGMATICALLY: *mysteriously*

She started at the question. "Ah, truly I had forgotten him! I am—"

"Thou hast had the business taken out of thy hands now, dame. Thou wert talking of Madge teaching a little knave to read when we came in, and Master Chaucer knoweth something of the child and his mother, and so 'tis settled he shall go and live near the spring of Holywell to drink the water, and have our Madge to teach him to read."

Margery was delighted at the idea of doing anything for so clever and learned a man as Master Chaucer; and when he promised to come sometimes and see what progress her pupil made, and tell them something of his travels, and the strange things he had seen in the countries beyond the sea, as a reward for their diligence, Margery thought herself the most fortunate and highly-favored girl in London.

Chapter V

Dame Ursula

SOFT May breezes had taken the place of the wintry winds, and spring sunshine was glowing on the budding leaves of the vines, and the apple blossom was making a goodly show in the orchards around what had now grown to be a fashionable suburban village—Holywell. So many invalids resorted to the spring at this season of the year that it was a very Bethesda[1], with halt, lame, and blind crowding to drink its waters and pay their devotions in the neighboring church. The Church reaped a rich harvest of votive offerings at such seasons as these, and kept a jealous eye upon such as were suspected of Lollardism, who yet dared to drink of this water, which the Church alone had the power to render curative in its effects.

There had been little difficulty in conveying Conrad and his grandmother to this fashionable resort; and his mother was with him, too, just now, for a short time; for the court had gone to Eltham

[1] A healing pool mentioned in John 5:2-4

HALT: *crippled*

VOTIVE OFFERINGS: *offerings of devotion*

Palace for a few weeks, or, rather, King Richard and his beloved bride had chosen to retire for a few weeks into the country, only taking with them a few of their usual attendants, so that half the court was now at Holywell, and nearly every house was full of visitors.

Master Geoffrey Chaucer had kept his promise, and Margery Winchester had kept hers, and was diligently teaching little Conrad to read. She found him an apt and intelligent pupil; but he puzzled her sorely by his strange questions sometimes.

"Mistress Margery, wilt thou tell me what this dreadful word Lollards doth mean—all it means?" he asked one day.

"Why? what hath this word to do with us or our reading?" she asked, scarcely knowing how to answer the boy.

"Because my grandam saith I shall certainly be a Lollard if I learn this reading; and there was a holy friar here yesterday begging, and he said if a Lollard ventured too near the holy spring it would boil up and scald him, and its waters, so good and healing to the faithful, would be changed into deadly poison by the evil that dwelleth in a Lollard, if he dared to drink it."

Margery smiled at the superstitious tale, and yet she hardly knew what to do—how to contradict it without betraying her own leaning toward the hated doctrine. "Did the friar tell you this himself?" she asked.

APT: *quick*

"Yes; I—I think my grandam told him to tell me the story for fear I should get 'tainted,' as she calls it, through learning to read, and that should hinder me from being cured."

"But it would not, Conrad; the waters will do you just as much good after you have learned to read as before. Perhaps the friar was mistaken about what he told you."

But Conrad shook his head. "My grandam said he could not have been mistaken. He was so holy and so dirty that—that I could hardly bear the sacred smell of his clothes. Was it a great sin to feel sick while he stood near me, and glad when he went away?"

"No, Conrad; you could not help feeling sick, I am sure; and God, who knows just how we feel, would not be angry at what we cannot help—what is natural to everyone who is cleanly in his ways. I think that the filthy habits of the friars are sinful rather than holy—indeed, I feel quite sure that they are."

"Oh, Mistress Margery, do not let my grandam hear you say this, or she will be so angry, for she says the dirty clothes of the friars are a proof of their holiness. Oh dear! what a puzzle this holiness is, too! I can't understand it at all; for, of course, the bishops are holy, more holy than the friars, or the Church would not give them so much power; and yet, instead of wearing a ragged, dirty old frock and cowl, and a rope girdle, like the friars, they wear splendid red and purple capes, embroidered with gold and costly stones. Now, how is it, Mistress Margery, that God can be so pleased with such different things—such filth and such riches? for they are alike holy, my grandam saith."

"I have learned that holiness is of the heart rather than of the outward appearance," said Margery, somewhat timidly; "'man looketh at the outward appearance,'[1] and it is to please man rather than God that bishops and friars display such luxury and such filth, my father saith. Bishops would not be suffered to go to court and dwell among the rich and powerful in the dirty clothes of a friar; while for the friars, if they were in no more sorry plight than the poor people, of whom they often beg, they would get but poor alms from any."

"Nay, nay! but thou art forgetting that 'tis God, and not man, these seek to please," said Conrad, quickly.

"I wot that if they sought to please God they would live less evil, selfish lives," said Margery, boldly.

"Nay, nay! speak not evil of bishops and priests, for 'tis next to reviling the holy father himself, and that were sin indeed—a sin as great as Lollardism," he added.

"Why art thou so afraid of Lollardism, seeing thou knowest so little what it is?" asked Margery.

"My grandam hath taught me to hate it; she says it is an evil worse than witchcraft, a sin greater

[1] I Samuel 16:7
SUFFERED: *permitted*
WOT: *know*

than all others; that—that—but you must keep this quite secret, Mistress Margery—that this evil of heresy hath made her life and my mother's most miserable."

"And thy mother—doth she hate it as fiercely?" asked Margery.

At this moment the door of the room was hastily pushed open, and Conrad, holding out his arms, uttered a scream of delight. "My mother! my mother!" he shouted; and the next minute he was folded in her arms.

Margery would have crept away, and left them to themselves, but the lady turned toward her as she rose from her seat. "Thou art Mistress Margery, I think," she said, in a pleasant voice; and she begged Margery to sit down again. "Accept my thanks for thy teaching," she said, eagerly. "I have often wished that my Conrad could learn to read; but my mother was so averse to it—so disliked the thought that he should ever learn the art—that, like a coward, I have feared to ask any to do it, lest it should vex her above measure."

"I have heard that Dame Ursula doth greatly dislike that any should learn this art," said Margery.

"Yes, yes; and it is no marvel, for she hath suffered much through it; we have all suffered, and must still suffer," she added, while a look of anguish came into her face; and then, for the first time, Margery noticed that the face, though fair and regular in feature, looked prematurely old, and there were lines of pain in it that only deep heart-anguish could have made, while among the abundant chestnut hair were streaks of grey that ought to have delayed their appearance for many years yet.

"My mother, when I have learned to read may I have the book the queen gave thee for me?" asked Conrad, in a half-whisper.

For answer the mother burst into tears. "What am I to do? What shall I do? I thought I had once settled all this forever—sacrificed all at the bidding of Holy Church and my mother—and that, having done this, the question would be forever at rest, and I should only have to beat down my own heart and keep it in its prison, where—But what am I saying?" she suddenly exclaimed, with an hysterical laugh, as Dame Ursula entered the room.

"Thou art late, Ermengarde," she said, somewhat sternly; "I have been watching for thee near the wooden cross, for I have somewhat to say to thee on a private matter."

"I will attend thee, my mother. Stay with Conrad until I return," she said, turning to Margery; and then she followed her mother to a little turret chamber, where they were safe from all intruders.

"Thou art ill, Mother," said Dame Ermengarde, as her mother sat down, panting for breath, as soon as the door was shut.

"No, I am not ill, and I shall not be ill until my work is done. Thou knowest what that work is,

Ermengarde?" Her daughter nodded, but could not trust herself to speak.

"Yes, thou knowest the task I have set myself to accomplish; and thou art trying to frustrate it," said Dame Ursula, in a measured tone.

"What have I done? what wouldst thou have me do more than I have done to prove my faithfulness to the Church? Oh, Mother, Mother, be merciful! I have crushed down my heart at thy bidding, and daily resist its strugglings still."

"And who brought all this struggle into our lives? Dost thou think thou art the only one that suffereth? But let us forget this. We have a work to do, Ermengarde, and we must do it; the stigma, the shame, must and shall be removed from our family, and our faithfulness to the service of the Church once more placed above suspicion."

Dame Ermengarde bowed her head. "I have promised to help thee in this thy heart's desire; what wouldst thou have me to do?"

"Send this wench away, this Mistress Margery!" she commanded.

"But, my mother, what hath she done?"

"She is teaching Conrad this hateful art of reading."

"And I thanked her for it but now; for if this holy spring should not cure Conrad, and he should be ever a cripple, this will help him to pass many an hour that else were weary and full of complaint."

"And is it not for the boy's sake I bid thee send the wench away? I tell thee she is more than half a Lollard, or the water Conrad hath drunk and hath rubbed into his flesh would have cured him ere now. It is her evil spells that turn aside the good the water would do, and, but for my constant prayers and penances, would turn it wholly to poison, I trow."

Ermengarde did not share her mother's superstitious fears, but she dared not disregard them altogether. "I do not think she will harm our Conrad," she said; "and it will, doubtless, do the child good to have something to think on besides his sore calamity."

"But this calamity must be removed; he will be cured; he must be, when the cause that brought this evil upon him is removed."

"And is it not removed? Are we not far enough? Oh, my mother!" And all Dame Ermengarde's firmness gave way, and she burst into a passionate flood of tears.

"Hush, Ermengarde, and yield not to such weakness! Doubtless the past hath cost thee some pain; render it not useless by refusing to do my bidding now."

"But, my mother, the water of this well hath been of little use to our Conrad; how, then, canst thou hope he will be cured by it?"

"Dost thou believe in the power of the saints to cure disease? Thou shalt believe ere long, and then, perhaps, thy wavering faith in the power of

PENANCES: *voluntary punishments for sins committed*

the Church will be renewed. Ermengarde, I am going on pilgrimage to the shrine of the most powerful saint in heaven, St. Thomas of Canterbury; surely, surely, he will hear my plea and cure our Conrad, for he hath a claim upon him through—" But there the old woman suddenly stopped.

Her daughter did not notice the abrupt pause, for she was lost in astonishment at what had been said just before. "You go on pilgrimage, my mother!" she slowly said, in a low voice.

"And wherefore should I not go?" demanded Dame Ursula.

"But you—in this strange country, of which we know so little, although we spoke its language before we came, and to which we are so closely united?"

"United! yes; Bohemia is united to England by this marriage of King Wenceslaus' sister to King Richard of England; but in no other way do I own that we are united!" said Dame Ursula, fiercely.

"But you said you had a right to the favor of St. Thomas because of—"

"Hush, Ermengarde! I forbid you to speak of this!" interrupted the old lady, almost trembling with passion.

It scarcely needed such a fierce command, for Dame Ermengarde was too much overcome by her own feelings, apparently, to say any more, and she sat and sobbed in silence for a few minutes. But, seeing the bitter, angry look in her mother's face, she subdued her emotion at last, and said, "Is it to secure Conrad's cure that thou art going to Canterbury?"

"Yes; I cannot trust to the water of the holy well after what I have heard from a friar who was preaching here last week."

"What hast thou heard, Mother?"

"Little more than I knew before; but I will tell thee, that thou mayest keep strict watch and ward over the child while I am gone, lest the evil thing come nigh him, and do him even more grievous harm."

"Thou knowest I would suffer no evil to come near my Conrad," said his mother.

"I trow not," replied Dame Ursula; "but since thou didst learn to call good evil, and evil good, thou art scarcely a judge in this matter, and therefore I say, keep all strangers from him, and especially this London merchant's daughter, this Mistress Margery, for she would not have learned this art of reading, I trow, were there not a book of the Scriptures to read, which thou knowest the Church hath forbidden."

Dame Ermengarde did not dare to tell her mother that she had in her possession the whole of the New Testament, as translated into English by Wycliffe, which had been presented to her by the queen for Conrad when he could read. She only said:

"But, my mother, hast thou seen Mistress Margery with a book of the Scriptures?"

"Seen it?" almost screamed the old woman,

STRICT WATCH AND WARD: *careful guard*

"dost thou think I would ever suffer the wench to come into my presence—ever to speak to the child again—if I had seen that? Nay, nay, I have not seen it, Ermengarde," said the old lady, more quietly; "but I suspect her, and I think she knows it. I watch her often, listen behind the arras, when she thinks I am far away."

"Oh, my mother, thou wilt not—"

"Dost thou not know what I would do? I tell thee the deed is a virtuous and noble one. Father Anselm, my confessor, saith that all deeds are pure and good, if done in the service of Holy Church; and surely she hath not a more faithful servant than poor old Ursula."

No; in this age of blind superstition and ignorance she had few slaves so blind as Dame Ursula; but that was not the fault of the Church. The light of knowledge she had effectually hidden; and liberty of conscience she was determined to strangle in its birth. It was a new thing in the world that England and Bohemia had dared to attempt—a few earnest souls, at least. That men should venture to think for themselves, or think otherwise than as the Church directed, was something so startling that at first neither pope nor bishops could believe it; but they were beginning to wake up to the danger with which they were threatened, and to realize that the new light and liberty must be crushed at all costs, and by all the means that they could command, either great or small.

Chapter VI

Going on a Pilgrimage

THERE was quite a commotion in the little village of Holywell when it became known that Dame Ursula was going on pilgrimage to Canterbury. Several others who had long been making up their minds to undertake the same pious errand, when the roads should be less infested with robbers, resolved to accompany her; for Father Anselm had arranged that she should join a large party of pilgrims, who were to meet at a hostelry in Southwark, and start from thence on their journey into Kent.

Dame Ursula wore a large cloak and a high-pointed headdress, in defiance of her daughter's advice that it would be better to lay aside this portion of her national costume, and wear a broad-brimmed hat, like the miller's wife, who was likewise to be one of the party. With them would ride a nun, the prioress of a neighboring convent, who was taking this journey partly for pleasure, partly for health, although she talked much of the

HOSTELRY: *inn*
PRIORESS: *head of the convent*

benefits her convent was to receive from the special intercession of the saint.

The Tabard Inn

Besides these three ladies there was a monk, a manciple, a yeoman, and a merchant of Chepe; and at the Tabard Inn, in Southwark, the general rendezvous for pilgrims going to Canterbury, a still larger party would meet them, to travel together for mutual safety and convenience. But they were not the only people riding forth from Holywell that fine spring morning, for a large party of friends were going with the pilgrims as far as the postern of London Bridge, and one of these was Master

MANCIPLE: *an official of a monastery or a college*
POSTERN: *gate*

Geoffrey Chaucer. He, with some other officers of the court, not being required to attend King Richard at Eltham, and his post of Comptroller of the Customs being almost a sinecure, was at leisure to spend a few days among the genial gossips gathered at Holywell; and what could be more pleasant than to ride through the country lanes of Holborn cracking jokes with the pilgrims, and giving them directions for their journey? This he was well able to do, for he had traveled in almost every country in Europe, and knew how to profit by what he saw passing around him.

"If Master Chaucer would but journey with us, our travel would be to more profit, I trow," said the monk, as he adjusted the gold brooch that fastened his cowl.

"Nay, nay, sir monk, thou mayest teach them to profit better than old Chaucer. What say you to telling them some legend or tale of what thou hast seen or heard in thy lifetime?"

"I know naught but the legends of my brethren the saints," said the monk.

"Ha, ha! thou wouldst have us believe that all monks and priests are saints, instead of sinners, as they are? But 'twill not do, sir monk; we can see the fox's nose peeping from under the cowl, and the wolf's tail from beneath the gown. Well, now, my honest yeoman, since the monk cannot teach thee, wilt thou not try to teach him? for I wot he knows but little except hunting and eating. What

SINECURE: *position requiring no real work*

sayest thou? hast thou a tale ready for this good company?"

But the yeoman laughingly shook his head, while the monk, seeing the laugh of everybody was turned against him, cast an angry look at Master Chaucer as he said, "If thou hast been in perils of travel, thou shouldst rather exhort these diligently to assoil their soul from all sin by true confession and penance, that if we come not to the shrine of the blessed Saint Thomas he may receive us into eternal rest."

"Nay, nay! what do we keep an army of lazy monks for, but to look after our soul's concerns for us?" said Chaucer, in a bantering tone; then, seeing that his words were likely to be taken too seriously, he added, "Do thy duty, sir monk, and exhort these people an thou wilt. I am a man of little wit, and can but tell a tale, which thing, I trow, any man can do; and so for the lightening of thy travel I should advise each one to tell a tale in turn as thou goest to Canterbury; and forasmuch as ye do part there, each one seeking a hostelry that best suiteth him, but are pledged to return together, ye shall relate as ye travel back all that befell ye in the city of the blessed saint."

Many smiled at the proposal, and thought it a good one; but that it should be carried out no one was willing to promise. Master Chaucer made his peace with the monk when he reached a vintner's near London Bridge, for the holy father

ASSOIL: *free*
VINTNER'S: *wine merchant's*

loved a stoup of red wine better even than a roast crane, and with a good draught of this to refresh him he now took the lead of the party until they should reach the Tabard; and the company of friends turned back toward the fields of Holborn, wondering when they should see the pilgrims return.

Among those who had accompanied them on this first stage of the journey were our old friends Masters Filpot and Trueman. They had walked beside the yeoman, and he was the bearer of sundry messages to old friends who had lived in the neighborhood of Canterbury twenty years before, and, therefore, were likely to be there still, unless death had summoned them away.

Besides these were Dame Ermengarde, who had gone thus far with her mother, listening to her directions and exhortations about the management of the house and little Conrad, until she felt a positive relief when the monk took his place at the head of the procession near London Bridge, and the palfreys of the three ladies slowly ambled after him.

At last she was free—free to breathe a sigh or shed a tear without being questioned and scolded; free to love her boy and show that love, and, better still, to talk to him without fear of her words being overheard and misconstrued. She wondered whether Conrad would miss her and look for her return, or whether he would be so taken up in mastering the difficulties of learning to read

STOUP: *cup*
PALFREYS: *saddle horses other than war horses*

that he would forget how long she had been away. Mistress Margery was with him, for she had summoned courage enough to refuse to send her away, although her mother had tried again and again, urging everything she could think of to induce her to separate Conrad from such a dangerous teacher as she chose to consider her.

She was still thinking of Conrad and Margery, wondering whether the girl was a Lollard, as her mother declared, when she was joined by Master Geoffrey Chaucer, who knew her as one of the attendants of the new queen.

"Now, prithee, if thou canst stay thy steps a little for an old man, I will bear thee company to Holywell. How is thy little knave, Conrad?"

Dame Ermengarde looked surprised at the question, for she did not know that Master Chaucer had been the active agent in the child's removal, or that he knew anything of him. Indeed, it seemed to her that he had assumed an altogether different character this morning; and she could scarcely recognize Master Geoffrey, the quiz and torment of the monk, as the quiet, thoughtful man who went about his duties when he was in the palace in a half-abstracted fashion, as though weightier thoughts were in his mind than dancing attendance on the king would be likely to give him.

He laughed merrily at Dame Ermengarde's perplexed look. "Thou didst not know that I had been to see thy little knave with my young gossip, Margery Winchester," he said.

MISCONSTRUED: *misunderstood*
PRITHEE: *I ask you*

"Thou dost know Margery Winchester—Mistress Margery, who is teaching my little Conrad to read? Then thou canst tell me whether my mother's fears are true or false. Is she—is she—"

But there Dame Ermengarde stopped. Perhaps she feared to have her own suspicions confirmed, and thus be unable to combat her mother's objections to the girl's visits when she should return.

Master Chaucer waited for her to finish what she was about to say; but finding she did not, he said, "I know not what Dame Ursula's fears may be concerning her, but she is a right proper maiden, and the daughter of an honest merchant living in the Chepe. Will that suffice thee, Dame Ermengarde?" he asked.

"Yes, yes; I am truly thankful for the service she hath done my little knave; and be she what she may, I—"

But here they were interrupted by the appearance of Master Filpot and his friend. No sooner did Master Geoffrey recognize the blacksmith than he said, "Here is another of thy son's gossips, Dame Ermengarde;" and then, turning to Filpot, he said, "This is little Conrad's mother."

The two, thus formally introduced, looked curiously at each other; and, indeed, they formed a strange contrast—the fair, fragile, worn woman, and the hale, hearty, happy-looking old man.

"And thou dost know my Conrad?" she uttered, in a tone of surprise.

HALE: *healthy*

"Ah! I know the little knave—learned almost to love him the first time I saw him," answered the blacksmith.

"That is no marvel, I trow, for thou dost love everyone except they treat thee worse than any dog!" grunted Trueman.

"Well, gossip, thou also wouldst love the little knave, I wot, if thou couldst see and hear him talk as I did."

"Ha, ha! but he would never set my old head aching after book-learning, as he did thine. Marry, it were a pretty tale to tell, that Filpot, the armorer, had forgotten the fashioning of cuirass and helmet, and taken to this new art of reading, that he might teach a little knave."

"Thou wert a right brave man to think of such a plan, Filpot," said Master Chaucer; "but the little knave learneth faster under the teaching of Mistress Margery, I trow. Thou seest, Dame Ermengarde, that many are anxious for thy little Conrad in this matter."

"I thank thee with my whole heart, gentle sir, for thy kind thought for my boy," said Dame Ermengarde, with emotion.

"Ah! thou dost owe it to worthy Master Filpot that Mistress Margery came to teach him this clerkly learning. Thou wilt come with us, Filpot, and see the little knave today."

"Nay, nay, Master Chaucer, I must to my smithy, I ween, now that I have seen the pilgrims fairly on their journey."

CUIRASS: *leather breastplate*
WEEN: *think*

"But I say thou must and shalt wend thy way to Holywell for this day at least. Thy friend shall come with thee, too; it will do the little knave good to see such a merry party. What sayest thou, Dame Ermengarde?"

"I shall be sorely grieved if these gossips refuse our request. I shall take it that they have grown tired of showing kindness to my little Conrad, or that they do not believe in his mother's gratitude for their kindness."

"Nay, nay, then; if thou wilt force us by such argument, we must come, I trow. Thou wilt go with me, Gossip Trueman?"

"Did I not say thou shouldst do with me as it best pleased thee for this one day?" growled out the mason.

"Ah! an' I will; and we will go to Holywell until sundown, and then go and tell Hugh Ryland how it fareth with Dame Ursula."

"As you like, as you like," grunted Trueman; and so it was agreed that they should spend the rest of the day with Dame Ermengarde and her little son, and that, if Mistress Margery had not gone, she should be asked to stay with them.

The little lame boy, so weak and helpless, seemed to exercise a sort of charm upon all who came near his couch. Learned Master Chaucer felt it almost as strongly as gentle Mistress Margery or kindly Master Filpot; but that the stern, rugged mason, Master Trueman, should yield himself wholly to

WEND: *make*

the same spell no one expected; and yet, strange to say, he seemed drawn to the child's side by a sort of fascination from the very moment that he first saw him.

When Mistress Margery left her place near his pillow, he at once seized the chance of taking it; and though he rarely spoke to the boy himself, he sat watching his face and listening to every word he said, with an eagerness that could not but be noticed by all who saw it.

Conrad's first question after his visitors were seated was, of course, about the pilgrims, and how his grandmother had borne her journey to London Bridge. "My grandam is sorely vexed in soul that the waters of the holy well have not cured me, or at least given me some strength in my legs and back," he said, with something of a sigh.

"And dost thou think this visit to Canterbury will do thee more good than the water?" asked Master Filpot.

"I know not what to think, for grandam hath been to Houndsditch, and given alms to the sick folk there, and besought their prayers. One hath promised to intercede with the holy virgin, sweet mother of mercy, for me; and another will pray to St. Thomas of Canterbury, who, they say, is the most powerful saint in England now; while another will beseech every saint she knows of; and hath done so, I doubt not; and yet it seemeth that the saints cannot or will not help me."

"They *cannot!*" said Mistress Margery, impulsively; "they have no more power to hear and answer prayer than I have."

Master Trueman stared at the speaker, as though he could not have heard aright; while the blacksmith sat and fidgeted on his stool, wishing Margery would be more cautious in what she said, and fearing that his old friend would be too much shocked ever to hear anything more of the new reformed doctrine that he was trying gradually to unfold to his mind.

Master Chaucer smiled as he said, "Art thou not fearsome of offending the saints by thy bold speech?"

"Nay, Master Chaucer; thou knowest that the saints were but men and women like ourselves, whom God helped to live holy lives, but never gave them power to answer prayer."

"Mistress Margery, what dost thou mean? What can we do, if the saints cannot hear us?" asked Conrad, anxiously; and the tears welled up to the boy's eyes, and his slight frame quivered as he spoke.

"God can answer prayer, Conrad," whispered Mistress Margery; "but we will talk of this another time;" and, fearing she had already said too much, she now rose to leave; and no one tried to prevent her departure.

Chapter VII

Was She a Lollard?

"MISTRESS MARGERY, wilt thou not tell me now of what thou didst say yesterday concerning the saints, and their not hearing our prayers?"

The subject had scarcely been absent a moment from Conrad's mind since the previous day; and he had trembled between hope and fear lest Margery's explanation should prove her to be one of those dreadful Lollards who talked of nothing but the heretic Wycliffe, and reviled the pope, and bishops, and everything that was holy.

This had been his grandmother's account of them; and it seemed that Margery was about to confirm its truth, and declare herself one of the hated sect by her statement concerning the saints.

"Margery, thou wilt tell me all—everything that thou dost believe. I asked the worshipful Master Chaucer what he thought thy meaning could be, after thou hadst gone; but he only shook his head, and said religion was growing to be a great puzzle.

Why should it be a puzzle, Margery, when we have so many to teach us all about it, popes and bishops, and monks and friars? why should it be a puzzle?"

"I don't know, unless it be that, there being so many teachers, they have grown idle, and from learning and doing little have come to learn or do nothing, except how they shall blind men to their ignorance while they follow their own pleasure."

"Did Master Chaucer tell thee that, Margery?"

"No; why shouldst thou think he did?"

"Because—but there, I do not know. Never mind Master Chaucer now; tell me what thou dost mean about the saints not hearing our prayers."

"I mean that they cannot hear our prayers, and we have no right to offer them to any but God Himself, or worship any but God Himself."

"But thou didst say they were holy, Margery."

"Yes, they were, mostly, men and women whom God helped to live holy, blameless lives; but we must not forget that they were men and women."

"But they are saints in heaven now; yet they remember all the pains they suffered here, and so can feel for us. Dost thou believe this, Margery?" asked Conrad, anxiously.

"We know not how much or how little the saints can understand of what is going on here. Of course, they would feel for us, if they could understand, and would help us, too, if they could."

"Then why cannot they? Oh, Margery, thou wilt not tell me that the saints cannot hear me pray—

that God will not let them hear!" exclaimed the boy.

"Conrad, suppose God should Himself listen to what thou art saying?"

But the bare suggestion of such a thing made the child shiver with a nameless fear and dread.

"I want the saints to hear me," he murmured. "My grandam saith that it is God who hath so sorely afflicted me; and so it is only the saints who can make me strong, and able to run about like other boys. I lie here thinking of it at night, and wondering what it must be to stand erect and feel the beautiful grass under my feet, and then I wonder why I cannot—why God hath so sorely punished me, and—and—I wonder what it is grandam talks about sometimes as the shame of our family."

The tears had welled into Margery's eyes as the boy spoke, and her voice trembled when she said, "Conrad, thou must try to think more of God's love."

"God's love!" repeated the boy; "nay, nay, Margery, how can He love me, and make me suffer so sorely? My mother loveth me, and longeth to see me well and strong, I know. My grandam loveth me, and hath gone to Canterbury for my sake, that I might be cured; and thou, wouldst not thou do me good?"

"Yes, yes; surely I would do anything that could give thee the strength thou needest," answered Margery.

"And the saints would doubtless help me if—if God would let them, Margery; but He will not, thou sayest; and how canst thou say He loveth me?" and Conrad burst into a flood of tears.

"Hush, Conrad! and let me try to explain something of how I think it is. God doth love thee, and it is because of this—because He loveth us so well, that He will not let the saints hear and answer our prayers. First, He would have us to know and love Himself, which we should not do if the saints were to come between. Suppose thou hadst never seen thy mother, but some others were allowed to do all that they could and would do for thee, and thou lookedst to them for all thou needst. Thou wouldst soon forget her, I trow, and her heart would be grieved—even as we grieve the heart of God when we pray to the saints instead of to Him. Then, too, the saints are not wise as God, nor do they know all that will come upon us, as He doth; and so, when we prayed to them to take something away because it hurt us, they might take from us just the best thing—just the very thing God hath given us because He loveth us and willeth to do us good."

"But, Margery, no one would ask the saints to take a good thing from us, I trow."

"We may not know that it is good; we may call the good thing evil, because we are not wise. When I was a little wench I fell down, and hurt my arm so sorely that a skillful leech had to be fetched; and he bound my arm up with some curious stones in the bandage, and very soon it began to hurt me, and I cried to my mother to take it off; but she was wiser than her little wench, and said, 'No.' My sister and the maids would have unfastened it at my piteous crying, not because they loved me more than my mother, but because they were not so wise or so patient to bear my passionate cries."

"But, Margery, this weakness cannot be good, like thy bandage or stones," said Conrad.

"We cannot see that it is good, because we are not wise as God, and we cry to Him and to the saints; and, perhaps, if they could help us they would; but they would spoil God's work in us, and the work, too, perhaps, that He means us to do in the world. And so God keepeth the help in His own hands, that we may seek Him only for it, and because we might wear out the patience of the saints by our impatient cries, and they should give us what we cry for, though it should do us harm."

Conrad shook his head sadly. Margery's words were "a hard saying,"[1] to him, and he could not receive it yet.

"Margery, hast thou ever thought that I shall never be able to do any work in the world—any man's work, I mean—unless I do get strong and receive the use of my limbs?"

"Thou mayest do God's work, Conrad—the work He doth mean thee to do—some special work that thou canst perform all the better for thy lameness."

[1] John 6:60

But the boy still shook his head. "The work for me—the only right work for me—is to take care of my mother and grandam. I have heard Father Anselm say it many times, and he would shake his head, and look at my grandam very hard. Margery, I wonder how it is I have not had a father like other boys. My grandam hath told me I never had one. Dost thou not think that God ought to have given the poor little lame boy a father?" he added.

"It may be that He did," murmured Margery; for she had not visited this strange household without noticing a good deal that would have escaped a less keen observer, and she had her own theory of Conrad's being fatherless.

"Thou dost think God did give me a father?" uttered Conrad.

Before this inconvenient question could be answered, Dame Ermengarde came in to say that a messenger had arrived, bringing a letter from Margery's father.

"Hath he come here for me?" asked Margery.

"Yes, he is even now at the door. Shall I bid him come to thee? for he seemeth to be in great haste."

Margery was quite impatient to see the messenger and hear the news he had brought, for she knew that something very unusual must have happened for her father to undertake the tedious task of writing a letter to her. It was not from the letter, but the messenger, that she expected to receive the most intelligence, for it was her father's most faithful and trusted apprentice, Gilpin, who had been sent, and she knew he would receive more in the way of messages to her than could be put in the letter.

"What hath happened, Gilpin? Is my mother well?" asked Margery.

"Yes, Dame Winchester is in good health, and my master, too; but sore trouble hath fallen upon them."

"Trouble?" and Margery started from her seat, exclaiming, "Surely no one hath—" she was about to say, "betrayed us," but the young man, understanding the direction her fears took, hastily interrupted her, for he had been warned by her friends that Dame Ursula was bitterly opposed to Lollardism.

"It is not anything thou canst have thought of," he said; "for Master Maryus has been beyond the seas for many years."

"My uncle hath come home at last—the brother my mother so often spoke of, and so longed to see!"

"Yes, he came back to her at last; but it was to die, Mistress Margery!" said Gilpin, in a gentle tone.

"To die? Oh, Gilpin! and I heard my mother say he had lived an evil, godless life—that he broke his mother's heart, and never knew of her forgiveness! Was he a different man when he came home?"

"I trow not, Mistress, for I heard the master say he loved and gloried in his wickedness; but, nathless, it hath made but little difference now, for he was rich, and hath left all his riches to the monastery of the black friars."

"And did he die thinking his riches would atone for his evil life?"

"Ah, what else could he think, when the friars promised him heaven, and the best place there, if he would only atone for the past by handing over all his wealth to them? They never left his bedside after they found out that he possessed riches; for before one brother departed another came; and when the master would have interfered and kept them out they accused him of wanting to ruin the sick man's soul. He was not satisfied with the leech, and would have sent for another from the white friars; but when they found that out they said Master Maryus was dying; and, by faith, he died the next morning—poisoned, my master saith," added Gilpin, in a whisper.

"And the friars have claimed my uncle's property!" said Margery.

"They have taken everything; he had two large chests full of money, and costly stones that he had gathered in his travels. But that is not the worst, Mistress Margery, for since he hath died his wife and two little children have come to my master, doubting not to find him there; and Dame Maryus hath herself fallen ill now, and is like to die."

"Oh, Gilpin, the poor little children! what will become of them? Surely the friars will give up what they have taken, now they have come."

"Nay, but they will not. They knew before Master Maryus died that he had left a wife and children beyond the sea, although the master had not been told; but they bade him think naught of wife or children now, but to save his own soul by devising to them all the moneys and riches he had in possession."

"'Tis cruel! 'tis unjust! 'tis robbing a widow and orphan children! Oh, Gilpin, they will surely restore half of what they have taken!"

"Nay, nay; not a single silver penny will they give up; and this poor foreign woman and her little children are wholly at the charges of thy father; and it is because of this—because, if trouble came, Mistress Margery, he would have little to pay the men of law to help him—that he bade me come hither and exhort thee to use discretion in thy speech at all times."

"Prithee, I thank thee, good Gilpin; and now tell me of thine own matters. Hast been to Finsbury Fields lately?"

"Ah, ah, Mistress Margery, I cannot give up this wrestling! 'Tis expected of all 'prentices that they should shoot with the arrow and wrestle without sark, and thou knowest the prize for the best wrestler—the ram and the ring; I have won it, Mistress Margery;" and the young man drew himself up with proud exultation.

"I am glad thou hast won it, Gilpin; but thou knowest the ram and the ring are not the only prize worth striving for."

DEVISING: *leaving*
SARK: *shirt*

"The ram and the ring are a small matter, I trow, as compared with another prize I hope to win," said Gilpin, with an animated look.

But Margery did not comprehend what he meant. "I would not have thee understand that I think we can earn our right to heaven," she said. "This 'grace of congruity' that the friars preach, leading men to trust in their own righteousness, instead of looking to Christ for salvation, is almost as bad as their teaching that we can make satisfaction for sin by penances, and then commute this by the payment of money, if we are rich."

"Ah, 'tis an accommodating thing, this religion that the friars preach. Thou must live purely, virtuously, and honestly, and thou shalt earn heaven, they say to one. Thou must do works of charity, visit the sick and infirm, and comfort the sorrowful, and thou shalt have a right to enter heaven, they tell to another. While for the rich, who will fain live in luxury and do whatever they list, they have this doctrine: Do thy pleasure and gain many riches, but give to abbeys and monasteries richly of all thy gains, and for these temporal gifts thou shalt have eternal life."

They had drawn nearer to Conrad while Gilpin had been speaking, but the rest of the conversation had been held in a recess, so that it should not be overheard; and that he had forgotten the caution he came to teach, Gilpin was altogether unaware until Conrad asked sharply, "Is thy speech

GRACE OF CONGRUITY: *grace given by God to someone whose actions have earned it*

WHATEVER THEY LIST: *whatever they please*

concerning the Church what this Wycliffe teacheth his Lollards?"

"I never heard Master John Wycliffe teach," answered Gilpin, promptly; "that which I affirm I have seen, and know to be the truth."

"Conrad, this is Gilpin, my father's 'prentice; and he hath won the ring and the ram for wrestling in Finsbury Fields," said Margery, anxious to turn the conversation.

But Conrad was not so interested in the account of Gilpin's success as he might have been at another time. What Margery had said to him, and what he had just heard from Gilpin, had set him thinking—wondering whether his grandmother might not be right, after all, in thinking that his teacher, Mistress Margery, and most of her friends, were Lollards.

TEMPORAL: *earthly*

Chapter VIII

The Earthquake Council

GILPIN had by no means exaggerated the danger that now menaced all the followers of Wycliffe living near London, for the Archbishop of Canterbury, Sudbury, having been murdered in the Wat Tyler rebellion, one of Wycliffe's fiercest opponents had been elevated to the vacant see. A few days before Gilpin's visit he had called together a court of doctors and bishops in the monastery of the friar-preachers, to lay before them certain doctrines repugnant to the Church; and several people known to hold these had likewise been summoned to appear. Wycliffe himself had been brought before a similar court under the former archbishop, but had escaped the punishment intended for him through the influence of his patron, the Duke of Lancaster, and the queen mother, Joan. But although Dr. Wycliffe himself was left in peace by his relentless foe, the archbishop was not likely to spare his followers; and Master Winchester was not likely to escape notice,

SEE: *region of authority*

especially just now, that he had made enemies of the black friars by trying to recover his brother-in-law's property from their grasp.

Happily for Margery's peace of mind, she knew nothing of what was passing at the monastery of the grey friars, for news traveled slowly in those days, and Gilpin had only given her the simple warning to be cautious.

But although Margery had not heard of this fresh outbreak against Wycliffe and the Lollards, others in Holywell had, and none were more alarmed than Dame Ermengarde; and she resolved to follow her mother's advice, and put an end to Margery's visits, for she more than suspected her of holding the dangerous doctrines of Wycliffe. But Conrad himself must be won over to see this matter in the same light; and so, as a bribe towards this, she promised to give him the book the queen had given her for him.

"Thou canst read now, my Conrad—read well enough to do without a teacher," she began one day; "and I will give thee the book my mistress hath given me for thee when thou hast time to read it."

"Time!" repeated Conrad. "I have time enough and to spare; wilt thou give me the book before thou goest back to the palace?"

"I will give it thee as soon as Mistress Margery hath left off visiting thee. Conrad, thy grandam was right; she is one of these Lollards, I doubt not."

Conrad looked troubled, but he could not contradict what his mother said, for, remembering that conversation they had had, and what he had heard from Gilpin since, he felt sure it was as his mother feared. But he was not going to betray his teacher by mentioning his suspicions even to his beloved mother; and he acquiesced in her wish that he should accept the book instead of Margery's visits, although it cost him a good deal of pain to be entirely separated from her.

Of this pain and sorrow that her pupil suffered Margery knew nothing, for Dame Ermengarde took care that she did not see him again. Very gently and very politely, and with many courtly phrases expressing her gratitude, but none the less unmistakably, did she tell Margery not to come again, as Conrad could not be allowed to see her any more.

Margery did not ask why she had been thus summarily dismissed. She thought Conrad had told his mother of their conversation. She did not know that the child was discreet beyond his years, and that he saw as plainly as she did his mother's weakness of character. This action of Dame Ermengarde convinced her that she was suspected as a Lollard; and, added to what Gilpin had told her, she resolved to be more cautious. She, too, felt the parting with Conrad, for she had grown to love the weak, afflicted boy, and she felt bitterly disappointed that she had not been permitted to give him further instruction in that knowledge which

ACQUIESCED: *yielded*
SUMMARILY DISMISSED: *dismissed without notice*

had been as new life to her. She could do nothing for him now, she thought—nothing but pray; and with the resolution never to forget the little lame boy when she prayed for herself, she returned to her home.

The return of the pilgrims from their journey to Canterbury caused almost as much sensation in the village as their departure. They had been expected some days before they came; and Dame Ermengarde was very anxious for her mother's arrival, for the court had returned to the palace at Westminster, and she ought to have returned to her duties there.

Dame Ursula was quite as anxious to get back as her daughter was to see her, for the journey had been very fatiguing, and she looked thin and worn, as well as travel-stained and weary.

But, in spite of her weariness, the old woman would not enter the house—would not alight from the horse on which she was riding—until she was assured that Margery was not there.

"I have met a holy friar, who hath told me much concerning these Lollards, and how they creep into houses, and stand beside the sick and dying, using all their arts to persuade them to give to them all the riches of which they are possessed, and they will save their souls."

If Dame Ursula had not been a foreigner, the friar would scarcely have dared to tell such a barefaced lie; for this practice with which he charged

BAREFACED: *shameless*

the Lollards was precisely what his own order was guilty of; and it was Wycliffe's exposure of this, and of their hypocrisy and evil lives, that had made them his bitter enemies.

"I have also heard other news. As I tarried at the Tabard on my way home, one told me of the earthquake that had shaken London of late. The monastery where the archbishop held his court that day to consider these doctrines of Wycliffe was shaken to its very foundations; and some of even the learned doctors were so far bewitched as to think that God would be displeased at the business they were doing. But the archbishop reproved such fears. 'If the earthquake means anything,' he said, 'it portends the downfall of heresy. For, as noxious vapors are confined in the bowels of the earth, and are expelled by these violent concussions, so through our strenuous endeavors the kingdom must be purified from the pestilential opinions of reprobate men.' But this is not to be done without great commotion. And there will be commotion, I trow, for of the conclusions these learned doctors met to consider ten are pronounced to be heretical, and fourteen erroneous and repugnant to the Church. This doctrine of the heretic Wycliffe, that the bread and wine in the mass are not changed into the body and blood of the Lord Christ, but are still simple bread and wine after the priest hath blessed them, no man dare teach now, for the truth of this hath been affirmed by a miracle."

PORTENDS: *foretells*
NOXIOUS: *poisonous*
PESTILENTIAL: *harmful*

Dame Ermengarde did not ask what this miracle was, for, in truth, she was utterly weary of this word "heresy," and her soul sickened as she listened to her mother's tiresome recital, for it brought back to her bitter memories of the past.

Conrad's mother might escape listening to the painful news that had been collected on the journey to and from Canterbury, but for him there was no escape. He had to listen to his grandam's account of what Archbishop Courtney was doing or had done for the repression of heresy.

"He is a man zealous for Holy Church, and hath obtained the king's patent to arrest and imprison all who shall publicly or privately teach or maintain these heresies of Wycliffe. He hath also obtained another patent directed to the chancellor and proctors at Oxford, appointing them inquisitors-general, and ordering them to banish from the university and town all who hold the heresies of Wycliffe, and all who shall even dare to receive into their houses Wycliffe himself or any of his friends. The heretic *must* leave Oxford now!" added Dame Ursula exultingly; "and when he can no longer corrupt men's minds by teaching them his evil heresies they will soon be forgotten, and the Church will be at peace once more."

"But, Grandam, hast thou forgotten what the friar told us one day—that there were hundreds of poor scholars traveling about the country teaching the doctrines of Wycliffe to all they met?"

REPROBATE: *wicked*
ERRONEOUS: *false*
PATENT: *permission*

"But these, too, will be imprisoned. I tell thee, Conrad, England is at last waking up to the danger of this heresy, and will cast it from her."

But Conrad, who was feeling very dull just now, and longed for a visit from Margery again, was somewhat perverse. "This Master Wycliffe is the orderly champion of English liberty, Grandam," he said.

"What hath the Church to do with liberty?" retorted the old lady; "she hath said what men shall believe; and no man dare think for himself in matters that concern the Church other than she shall direct, even though he be the professor of divinity chosen by the University of Oxford, and hath for his patrons queens and dukes. This Wycliffe must wend his way from Oxford, I trow, and no man dare receive him into his house—so that he will die, as it is meet he should, begging for food and shelter that none will give him."

Dame Ursula doubtless hoped that her prediction concerning Dr. Wycliffe would speedily be fulfilled; but Conrad had begun to tire of her endless talk about heresy and heretics, and wished he had never heard the word, since it had separated him from Margery. Not that he needed much assistance from her now in the way of teaching, for he had learned so rapidly, and had applied himself so strenuously to overcome every difficulty, that he could master the contents of the book his mother had given him before she took her

PERVERSE: *contrary*

departure. Dame Ursula could not read herself, and little guessed that the book she so often placed near Conrad's pillow was the hated Wycliffe's Testament in English. Dame Ermengarde knew what the book was, but as the queen read it so much she reasoned that it could not be other than good for Conrad to read; but she took care not to let her mother know what it was.

The old lady began to watch for some signs of amendment in her grandson as soon as she returned from Canterbury; but, in spite of the constant use of water from the holy well, and the prayers and gifts she had offered at the shrine of St. Thomas, he did not improve. On the contrary, as the summer advanced he seemed to grow more weak and helpless, and became so irritable and peevish that Dame Ursula gladly welcomed any visitor who would spend an hour with him.

The blacksmith came sometimes, when he could leave his smithy for a few hours; but his friend Trueman often came to talk to the little lame boy; and each time he came he felt his heart drawn more closely toward him. No one was so patient in listening to his complaints or trying to amuse him as the cross-grained old mason. Indeed, the man's whole nature seemed to change when he was with the boy, and he entered into all his schemes and plans for the future with as much sympathy as though he were a boy himself.

"Master Trueman, I will be a learned man—a

AMENDMENT: *improvement*
PEEVISH: *cross*
CROSS-GRAINED: *stubborn*

learned doctor—so that men shall call me the 'seraphic doctor,' and thou must help me," said Conrad one day when his friend came in.

"Ah, that will I right heartily, my little knave," said Trueman, rubbing his hands; "I have heard that if Englishmen were only learned they would be free—free to own the land without paying body-service, and—"

"And free of the Church, too, I have heard," laughed Conrad; for since the Church had failed to give him the health and strength he so longed for, he had less fear of what he said concerning it.

"Ah, I know little of the Church beyond paying all dues and relieving the begging friars when they ask an alms; though 'tis a sore tax on a poor man to pay Church dues and give of his substance continually to these holy beggars, for the land swarms with them, I trow."

"My grandam hath given alms to two today and three yesterday. One of them today was a grey friar, whose monastery was far away in the west of England; and he sat awhile to rest, and told me of a monk of his order, one Roger Bacon, who died about ninety years ago. He was a most learned man, he says, and could tell much concerning the stars and a science called mathematics; but he was never called a 'seraphic doctor,' I trow, for he offended the Church because of his great learning, and they imprisoned him, as they imprison the Lollards now. Doth the Church hate learning

SERAPHIC DOCTOR: *literally "an angel-like teacher;" a title given to Saint Bonaventure, a thirteenth century theologian* because it tendeth to liberty, think you, Master Trueman?"

But the mason could only shake his head. He was not going to speak against the Church and imperil his good name—perhaps lose his dearly loved liberty—for in these uncertain times none knew how much power the Church really did possess in disposing of men's bodies as well as their souls.

But Conrad was weighed by no such fear, and he said so. "I would be a Lollard, and pray to God Himself, as Mistress Margery doth, if I were sure I should get well and run about like other boys," he said.

"Be cautious, little knave, what thou dost say about that, for 'tis growing more dangerous every day to be a Lollard, I trow."

"Well, I will not tell my grandam, for it would trouble her sorely. But now about this learning; thou must ask some of thy friends to lend thee some books for me to read, for I mean to be a 'seraphic doctor,' well-skilled in the use of words, that I may confuse and confound all who think differently from me."

Trueman smiled at the eagerness with which the boy spoke. "Dost thou think I see as many books as stones, that thou askest me to get thee books? Nay, nay, poor old Ned Trueman hath not beheld half a dozen books in his life; but if thou wilt have this learning thine heart is set upon, ask Master Geoffrey Chaucer, and he will be able to help thee,

I doubt not. But I—" and the old man stopped to laugh at the absurdity of the idea.

But, strange and unlikely as it seemed to him then, the next time he came to see Conrad he brought a book with him. He did not tell the boy he had given a day's work for the loan of the book, neither had he inquired what the book was. Conrad wanted books to learn the use of words—to become a scholar, as the word was understood then—and any book would be useful, he argued; and so he joyfully brought the coveted storehouse of words—for it was words rather than knowledge that were coveted in those days.

The philosophy of Aristotle was most carefully studied; and this, with the prevailing ignorance of the times of which we write, helped to confuse men's minds, but added very little to the lightening of the general darkness. Polemical weapons were furnished to disputants, but no useful truths were made known. Endless questions were started, but as it was a mark of skill and knowledge to ask these, without attempting to furnish an answer or seek one, and as no one ever thought of answering questions, but only asking them, very little useful knowledge was gained, or even sought; and the more skilled in this art of asking questions and disputing gained the title of "seraphic." And to be a "seraphic doctor" was now Conrad's highest ambition.

POLEMICAL WEAPONS: *controversial arguments*

Chapter IX

The Disabled Traveler

CONRAD seized the book eagerly, and, looking at the title, he exclaimed, "Thou wilt have me to dispute with the Lollards, I trow!"

"Nay, nay! leave the Lollards alone," said the old man. "This book hath naught to do with them, I wist."

"Naught to do with them! Why, 'tis writ by Master Wycliffe!" and Conrad read from the title, "*Against Able Beggary, Against Idle Beggary,* and *On the Poverty of Christ.*"

"Now, by my faith, if I had known that the book was of that sort I would not have brought it!" uttered Trueman, in a tone of perplexity. "I thought, being a book, it must be good, and now—"

"Nay, nay, I am not going to be a Lollard, Master Trueman; I mean to be a 'seraphic doctor.' Shall I read to thee something from this book? 'Tis about the monks and friars."

Master Trueman thought he might as well hear what kind of learning the book contained, and if

WIST: *know*

it threatened to be too dangerous he would take it back again. But Conrad would not hear of this; he would not part with the book, but promised that his grandmother should not know its contents; and with this promise the old man was obliged to be content; but he resolved to come again soon and fetch the dangerous treasure, for he would know no peace while Conrad had it, for fear it should bring trouble upon them all.

But the child kept his word, and no one knew he had the book but his grandmother, and she knew nothing of its contents. She felt so bitterly disappointed that all her efforts had failed to restore him some degree of strength, that she was glad of anything that would amuse him now, and make the time pass less wearily; and it was for this reason she welcomed every visitor who would come to pass an hour with the boy. Even Master Filpot, the blacksmith, was welcomed less sourly, although she felt sure he was one of the detested Lollards.

Master Geoffrey Chaucer could not spare time to come to Holywell very often, but whenever he did journey thither he never failed to pay a visit to Conrad, and tell him something of his travels in other countries; and he often lent him a book to read. Such books as those of Master Chaucer, as well as that brought by Trueman, were scarcely likely to interest an ordinary child; but the peculiar circumstances in which Conrad was placed made him welcome anything that could occupy his mind, and draw it from the painful subject of his affliction.

That he was strangely thoughtful for his years was only natural, for, being cut off from all the usual active amusement of boys of his age, his mind was thrown back upon itself, and he not only read every book he could obtain, but thought far more of what he read than did many older people.

Weeks and months rolled on, and Conrad's mind was being stored with all sorts of different kinds of knowledge, mostly of a controversial character; for everyone who wrote seemed bent upon pulling down some theory or contradicting some received opinion; but no one ever thought it necessary to repair or rebuild as well as pull down, so that Conrad, like everybody else, began to look out for things to find fault with. That the Church, with all her boasted power of healing and working miracles, had failed to cure him, was a never-failing source of complaint; while to Dame Ursula it was a grief that threatened to undermine her health entirely.

In the spring of the year 1384 it was proposed to Dame Ermengarde that Conrad should try a change of air, for he had been nearly two years at Holywell, and the water had done him no good. Of course, anything that was likely to be of service to the boy was eagerly sought by his mother, and no less eagerly by his grandmother; and so preparations were at once made for their removal to a small village in Leicestershire, close to Lutterworth, where an old retainer of the Duke of Lancaster had settled, who agreed to receive Dame Ursula and her grandson into his house.

The excitement of taking such a journey, and seeing so many strange people and places, seemed to have a most beneficial effect upon the boy; and although he could not walk, he was so much stronger that soon after his removal to Leicestershire he was able to go to church for almost the first time in his life.

Dame Ursula was delighted that Conrad should wish to go to church, and eagerly proposed that he should go to mass while he was able; and to this Conrad agreed, for he would be sure of heaven then, and it would please his grandmother, too. Indeed, Dame Ursula was so delighted at what she chose to consider Conrad's escape from Lollardism, and his devotion to the Church, that she could not help openly exulting over it. But she soon found that Conrad was not likely to receive all that the Church taught and practiced as unquestioningly as she did.

"Grandam, why doth the priest only take the wine in the mass?" he asked, as soon as he returned home; "at Holywell the people as well as the holy father took wine as well as the bread."

"But hast thou not heard, my Conrad, that the wine taken by us common people remains simply wine, but that which the priest taketh is changed into the blood of Christ?"

"Then why cannot we partake of this wine that is changed, instead of taking only the bread?"

"Because it is not needful, for the bread is changed into the flesh and blood of Jesus Christ. Didst thou not hear of the knight who almost believed in this heresy of the Lollards, that the bread is not so changed, until a miracle was performed, and after the priest had blessed the bread he saw it to be red, raw flesh, dripping with blood. This miracle was performed just after the Earthquake Council was held in London, where Wycliffe's doctrine was condemned."

But Conrad was not quite satisfied. "I heard my mother say that the mass should be taken in both kinds," he objected.

"Thy mother hath some strange notions, which it were well for thee to forget. Dost thou not see for thyself, Conrad, that if the wine were turned into the blood of Christ, there would be sore peril of its profanation, for it might be spilled in delivering the cup to the hands of so many?"

Conrad was silenced, but not satisfied, and he resolved to talk to his host about this. He also had a lurking desire to go with the old man to Lutterworth Church, to hear Master Wycliffe preach sometimes, for he had never heard anything in the way of preaching but a recital of the legend of some saint gabbled over by an ignorant monk

PROFANATION: *violation*
GABBLED OVER: *muttered*

or friar; for, although a canon had been enacted about a hundred years before, making it incumbent on a parish priest to explain the fundamental articles of religion once a quarter, this was often neglected through the ignorance of those to whom it was entrusted.

At Lutterworth, however, things were quite different, for Dr. Wycliffe was as earnest and diligent as a parish priest as he had been when the Oxford professor of divinity, and he was scarcely less useful either, for the "poor scholars," who had often heard him preach and lecture there, followed him to Lutterworth, often bringing with them noble patrons, to whom they had hired themselves as teachers.

One of these poor scholars came to Master Martin's cottage one day, and begged a night's lodging for himself and his master, Sir John Oldcastle. They were on their way to Lutterworth, but the young nobleman had met with an accident; his horse, having stumbled in the rutty, ill-kept road, had thrown Sir John into a ditch and sprained his foot.

Master Martin scarcely liked to turn away any travelers under such circumstances, but he had not a room to spare now, and this he explained, but added, "I will ask the old lady if she will sleep with my dame tonight, and thou couldst have her bed. There is a little lame knave with her; but he will count for naught, as he sleepeth on the couch he lies on by day."

CANON: *church law*
INCUMBENT ON: *an obligation or duty of*
ONCE A QUARTER: *every three months*

Sir John Oldcastle meets with an accident.

"If the woman will but do this kindly deed for my master he will reward ye both," said the man, as Martin turned into the house to speak to Dame Ursula.

The thought of this unknown traveler being lamed, perhaps, by his fall, moved the old lady at once, and she readily consented to give up her bed, if Conrad would not mind being left with the strangers; and the boy, so far from disliking the idea of it, was delighted, more especially when he heard that one of them was a poor scholar, who had recently come from Oxford.

He had begun to perceive lately that if he was ever to become the great scholar he wished to be, he, too, must go to the university; and he thought this man might tell him something of what was done there, and how the students learned their great wisdom.

Sir John Oldcastle had injured his foot rather severely, it seemed, for he could not walk to the cottage, and had to be laid on Dame Ursula's bed at once; and when the long piked shoes which he wore were taken off, the injured foot was found to be very much swollen and inflamed.

The shoes, with their yard length of toes, that had been loosely drawn up to the knees with silver chains, had been the chief cause of the disaster, and Sir John declared he would never try to be a fashionable young man again.[1] In truth, his gay attire looked in a sorry plight now, for it was quite

[1] Years later, a law was passed limiting the length of the points on these shoes to 11 inches. The penalty included being cursed by the church and several fines.

unfit to travel in; but the lad—for he was little more than that—had been so pleased with the effect of having one sleeve blue and the other green, one cloth stocking red and the other white, to say nothing of the gold and silver tissue embroidered round doublet and tunic, that he could not be persuaded to lay aside his gay court dress when he left London, and dress in a more sober fashion.

The finery was sadly torn and mud-stained now, and Sir John was ready to curse his folly and vanity alike; but he restrained his impatience, for he would not grieve his companion.

Conrad lay quietly, looking and listening to all that passed, while the injured foot was bathed and bandaged; and after they had retired to rest and forgot all about Conrad, he still lay wide-awake, breathlessly listening to every word; for Sir John could not sleep for the pain his foot caused him, and so he and his companion lay talking until near day-dawn.

It seemed that Sir John's character by no means accorded with his foppish dress, for Conrad soon discovered that it was not the court and the gay doings of King Richard that had occupied the young men's attention while in London, for they had been making inquiries about a Lollard who had been condemned to imprisonment for life—one John Ashton. They had not seen him, it seemed, for he had died the year before from the closeness of his confinement.

DAY-DAWN: *dawn*
FOPPISH: *vain*
CLOSENESS: *oppressiveness*

In spite of this warning, which Conrad thought would be enough to deter any man from embracing Lollardism, it seemed that not only the poor scholar, but Sir John Oldcastle also, had a strong leaning in that direction, and had journeyed hither to hear Master Wycliffe himself.

But it was not of Wycliffe alone that they talked. The scholar, while at Oxford, had visited the cell of Roger Bacon, and knew an old monk who had been his intimate friend.

"This Bacon had many curious things, which his friend showed me. There were glasses, to help men to see more clearly whose eyesight was not good, and others by which the most distant stars were brought within sight—"

"Surely the man must have had dealings with Sathanas. 'Tis of the evil one that these inventions come," said Sir John.

"So said the Church, as it saith of all learning and useful knowledge; and the poor monk was soon carried from his cell to a gloomy dungeon. But they brought him back before he died. His friend doth greatly reverence him, and saith he will yet be called the father of English philosophy. This man also knew John Duns Scotus, who was the professor of divinity at Oxford, but saw not so clearly the evils of the times and the Church as doth our godly Master Wycliffe. The old monk was a friend, too, of William Occam, the 'invincible doctor,' who was one of the first to show men the

SATHANAS: *Satan*

errors of the Church, and how greatly it needed to be reformed. He and Thomas Bradwardine, some time Archbishop of Canterbury, and known as the 'profound doctor,' would sit in old Roger Bacon's cell and examine his instruments, and listen to what his friend told concerning him, and read his books, until Thomas Bradwardine grew to love the mathematics and philosophy of Bacon as much as he did the divinity lectures of his teacher, Duns Scotus."

"But none of these are equal to our Dr. Wycliffe, thou sayest."

"No man hath ever seen so clearly as Master John Wycliffe the evils and corruptions of the whole Roman Church, and how greatly it needs to be reformed."

"But who is to reform it?" asked Sir John Oldcastle. "The Church and the world, as it seemeth to me, need a reformation, and men have been crying and struggling for it for years; but will it ever come?"

"Yea, in God's time it will," answered the poor scholar.

"Thou sayest we ought ever to hope in God, and believe that His long tarrying is but His patience and longsuffering; but it seemeth to me that evil is the stronger in our day, and will yet get the upper hand. Thou knowest I more than half sympathized with that foolish rebellion headed by the blacksmith, Wat Tyler; for was not that a noble struggle for freedom—the world striving to cast off the chains that had been riveted upon it by the kings and barons and men of power? And now thy Wycliffe would fain free men from the slavery that the Church hath imposed upon all; but he is silenced—sent from Oxford in disgrace—and the Church is rejoicing in her power to persecute and crush all who dare to preach or teach, or even believe the doctrines he taught. With such things as these before us, how are we to hope that a reformation will ever come—that men's wrongs will be redressed, and freedom to worship God according as the heart teacheth ever granted to men?"

"Truly, as thou sayest, all things look dark and menacing for the future; but the world hath been groaning and crying for a reformation for many years, and it will still cry, and God will hear the voice of His servants praying, 'Lord, how long?'[1] and the reformation will come; and we must hope in the Lord until this glorious day shall dawn on the earth."

[1] Psalm 6:3

REDRESSED: *made right*

Chapter X

New Friends

CONRAD lay as wide-awake as Sir John Oldcastle himself, and so he heard every word that was spoken by the two friends; and they gave him new thoughts, new ideas upon many subjects, especially this much-reviled Lollardism. If the world and the Church wanted setting to rights, as his grandmother said the house did sometimes, why, it had better be done; and if Dr. Wycliffe had found out the way to do one part, it seemed a pity that he could not be left alone, or helped to do the work he wanted to do. One thing he was quite resolved about—he would go to Lutterworth Church and hear Dr. Wycliffe, if old Martin would take him, in spite of all his grandmother might say against it. He stood in far less awe of the old lady than did his mother; indeed, it seemed that in some particulars Dame Ursula and the boy were strangely alike, and it was doubtful which would gain the victory if their wills came in direct collision.

The travelers were anxious to proceed on their journey with as little delay as possible; but the young nobleman's foot was still so much swollen that their host declared it was impossible for him to move at present. He chafed and fumed a good deal when he heard this, and declared he must go on as far as the town, and would have sent his friend forward to engage rooms for them at some hostelry, but that the poor scholar persuaded him to remain where he was.

Conrad was delighted at the thought of sharing his room with such company, and Sir John soon became reconciled to his enforced confinement, when he discovered what a quaint, original companion he was likely to have in the little lame boy; for Conrad's miscellaneous reading had helped him to understand the full meaning of the first conversation that he had overheard, while that had given him a clearer insight into the drift of much that he had failed to understand in the books.

"So *thou* wouldst be a reformer, my little knave!" said Sir John Oldcastle, after one of their conversations.

"Nay, I know not that, for to me it seemeth the world will not be set to rights, though men be willing to use their besoms."

Sir John laughed at the homely simile. "Ah! truly, one or two have tried their besoms, but only, as it seems to me, to raise a cloud of dust instead of cleansing away the filth and foulnesses."

BESOMS: *brooms*

"Will preaching and teaching ever do more than raise a dust, and fill men's nostrils with a foul scent?" said Conrad, recalling to mind his grandmother's last housecleaning, when the rushes, dirt, and putrid bones and scraps, the accumulation of the previous six months, had been swept out of the room, and the disagreeable business had well-nigh made him sick.

"Thou dost think men will grow disgusted with the teaching of Dr. Wycliffe?" said the nobleman.

"Lollardism doth stink in men's nostrils now," said Conrad. "To be a Lollard is to forfeit the favor of prelates and nobles, and all whose favor is worth having."

"But if the world is to be reformed some must be willing to offend prelates and nobles; for 'tis through them, I trow, it is in such bad case."

"Nay, nay; but 'tis the work of the prelates to reform the Church!" said Conrad.

"And dost thou think they will do it?" exclaimed the young nobleman. "I tell thee their hearts are set on their green and scarlet gowns, their gold embroidered copes, and such finery, as much as any young damsel of Queen Anne's court is upon the height of her horned headdress or the width of her gored skirt. 'Tis a Bohemian fashion, I trow, this newfangled headgear."

"Yes, I came from Bohemia," said Conrad.

"I knew thou wert not an English boy. Didst thou ever hear of one Master Faulfisch in thine

PRELATES: *high church officials*
COPES: *long cloaks worn for processions*
HORNED HEADDRESS: *a headdress with a supporting frame*

own land?" asked the poor scholar.

But before Conrad could reply in the negative his grandmother came into the room and took up the question.

"Faulfisch!" she repeated. "They are our kinsmen. What dost thou know concerning them?"

"I knew one Master Jerome Faulfisch at Oxford, who came from Bohemia," said the scholar; but he wisely kept back another item of news concerning him—that he had come to Lutterworth to see this Bohemian, and to consult with him as to the best method of introducing more of Dr. Wycliffe's doctrines into Bohemia. They were to talk the matter over with Dr. Wycliffe himself, for Faulfisch, having studied at Oxford under him, and read his works, was very anxious that his countrymen should receive the light of Divine truth from Wycliffe, and participate in the blessing God was giving to England.

"So Jerome Faulfisch hath come to England?" repeated Dame Ursula, musingly.

"Thou wouldst be glad to see thy kinsman, I trow?" said Sir John Oldcastle.

"Nay, nay; I have no desire to see him. Thou wilt not say thou hast seen me," she added, a little anxiously.

"But, Grandam," said Conrad, "I would fain see this Bohemian scholar. I prithee let him come hither, for I have often longed to see someone who came from Bohemia since ourselves."

But a stern, hard look came into Dame Ursula's face, and she answered angrily, "Nay, the man shall not enter this house!" and then, recollecting herself, she added, "He could tell us naught of our former gossips, Conrad, for he left Prague long before we came to England."

Conrad did not like to say anything more about the matter before these strangers; but he was none the less desirous of seeing Master Faulfisch, and he resolved to ask at what hostelry he was staying before the travelers should take their departure, and having ascertained this, he would ask old Martin to take him there when they went into town. Conrad found that the strangers were willing to give him all the information he desired, and Sir John proposed that he should go with them to Lutterworth.

"Hast thou never tried to walk on crutches?" asked Sir John, as he tried himself to hobble across the room by the aid of two sticks.

"Nay, I cannot sit up long but the weakness overpowers me," said Conrad, with something of a sigh, as he watched Sir John's successful efforts to move about. The young nobleman himself was delighted at the progress he made with the help of the sticks. "If I could get something to rest upon under my arms, I could go to Lutterworth today;" and then he suddenly added, "I will ride thither, and get some crutches made, and when I have done with them I will send a litter to fetch thee, and thou shalt try and walk with them, and see thy kinsman Faulfisch, and Dr. Wycliffe too."

Conrad would fain have jumped for joy at the prospect of going to Lutterworth; but the distant pleasure was somewhat dimmed by the present pain of losing Sir John Oldcastle and the poor scholar. They had been a week at the cottage now. A week of almost uninterrupted pleasure it had been to Conrad, for Sir John, having resigned the hope of going on to Lutterworth at once, resolved to make the best of his imprisonment; and, like everybody else who came in contact with the little invalid, he was so charmed and interested by him that he gave himself up to his amusement at once, and the days had slipped by almost as quickly to one as to the other.

But for the hope of seeing his friends again so soon, Conrad would almost have pined and fretted for them after they had gone. Dame Ursula, having overheard several fragments of conversations, guessed that they were tainted with Lollardism, in spite of the gay attire in which Sir John Oldcastle had first made his appearance, and which the old lady had taken as a sure indication that he might certainly be trusted, as being free from all suspicion of heresy; but now, finding that they were going to Lutterworth to see Dr. Wycliffe, she set about the work of trying to remove any impression they might have made upon Conrad.

"But, Grandam, if this so-called heresy is what the Church needs to set it right again—for it seemeth that it hath gone wrong of late—then—"

But Dame Ursula interrupted him with a cry of horror. "The Church wrong!" she uttered; and then she wrung her hands, and burst into such a cry of anguish that Conrad was alarmed, and called old Martin into the room.

"What aileth thee, dame? what is it, my little knave?" asked the old man.

But Conrad hardly knew what to say. "I—I am afraid I said something that hurt grandam," he answered, hesitatingly.

Dame Ursula took no notice of old Martin, but continued to rock herself to and fro, groaning, "Oh, my boy! my boy! he is lost! lost! lost!"

"Nay, good dame, thy son may come home to thee again," said Martin, soothingly, for he could not think that anything Conrad had said could cause this violent outburst; and so he went on talking soothingly to her, until at length, finding she paid little heed to what he said in a soothing tone, he spoke more sharply. "'Tis an evil thing to turn a deaf ear to the counsel of a friend; and thou art not the only one who hath lost a son. 'Tis a sore grief, I know, dame, for my own brother is in the same case, and he hath buried himself in London ever since. He was a right clever mason, was my brother, Ned Trueman, and—"

"Trueman!" interrupted Conrad, "I know a Master Trueman, who is also a mason; but I knew not that thy name was Trueman," he added.

"All men called me Martin when I entered the service of the great duke; and my brother was so sorely offended at my rendering body-service to any man that he hath not spoken to me since, for he never forgiveth an offense."

"Never forgiveth!" repeated Conrad.

"Nay, he would not forgive his own son, though he was his only one, and he loved him dearly; and 'twas this that sent the knave away. He went beyond the seas; and my brother went to London to forget his sorrow if he could; but I doubt not that he hath often grieved since and will grieve even to the last. So think not, dame, that thou art the only one who hath lost a son."

Dame Ursula had grown more calm while old Martin was speaking—calm enough to reflect that it would be better to let old Martin think he was right in his conclusion as to the cause of her trouble than compromise Conrad by telling her fears concerning him. If she had only known that the old man would have laughed at her gross exaggeration of the danger, she might have told him the true state of the case, for she would have been thankful to anyone who would have told her she had little to fear. As it was, she let old Martin depart with the belief that she was grieving for the loss of a son, while she again commenced her lectures to Conrad on the enormity of his sin in doubting the wisdom, goodness, and righteousness of the Church in any particular.

The effect of his grandmother's talk this time was to make Conrad think she knew nothing of the world's cry for the reformation that Sir John Oldcastle had talked so much about; and though he tried to soothe her with promises that he would never do anything against the Church—promises she felt inclined to laugh at—he would not promise the entire obedience to her she had always extorted from him before.

"Grandam, I shall be a man someday. I am growing a man every day, it seemeth to me; and as I cannot work like other men, I must think. I have strange thoughts sometimes, Grandam; and I must know more of what this Sir John hath told me about the groaning of the world for a reformation. I must go to Lutterworth when he sendeth for me, Grandam, for it may be I shall be able to walk when—"

"Hush, hush, Conrad! these Lollards have bewitched thee. Dost thou think this heretic, Wycliffe, can give strength to thy legs, when St. Thomas himself hath failed?"

"Nay, nay, Grandam; I said not that Dr. Wycliffe would do aught for me but let me hear his voice when he preacheth to the people in Lutterworth Church."

"Thou shalt not go to Lutterworth!" said Dame Ursula, angrily.

"Nay, nay, Grandam, say not so, for I would not disobey thee an I could help it; but I am growing to be a man, and have not child's thoughts now, and I must go to Lutterworth when Sir John Oldcastle doth send for me;" and Dame Ursula, looking at the pale, thin face, saw that it would be useless to try to rule and reign over this boy as she had ruled and tyrannized over his mother.

"Thou mayest go to Lutterworth once—go and see this heretic, Wycliffe; and I will pray the saints that thou art not blinded by the evil that is in him, for he hath blinded many souls, and ruined them forever."

The consent was given reluctantly enough, Conrad could see; but he was glad that he had obtained her consent so far; and he resolved that he would not stay in Lutterworth more than a few days, however much his new friends might press him to do so. No, no; he would not leave his grandmother long. He was beginning to understand her now, and comprehend something of the absorbing love she had for him, and the intense fear that was ever on the alert against anything like heresy. He knew, too—though how he knew it he could not tell—that there was some mystery connected with this fear—some secret—something that had happened in the past that seemed ever present to his grandmother's mind, making her restless and irritable, unless she had her rosary in her hand, reciting the prayer appointed for each bead, or some such act of devotion.

ROSARY: *a string of prayer beads*

He had tried again and again to penetrate the mystery in which the past seemed to be shrouded. He had asked questions about their life in Bohemia—why his mother always looked so careworn and anxious, when and where his father had died, what he was like, and whether he had loved his little lame boy. But to all his questions Dame Ursula only returned evasive, unsatisfactory answers—answers that silenced Conrad for the time, but never satisfied him. Now he resolved to question another. He would see this Master Faulfisch, whom his grandmother said was a kinsman, when he went to Lutterworth, and he would question him about his father and the mystery that seemed to enfold his family.

Chapter XI

Jerome of Prague

CONRAD had not to wait long for his summons to Lutterworth. A week after his departure Sir John Oldcastle sent a litter, in which the lame boy could be carried to the hostelry where he was staying, and where he was most anxious to see Conrad make trial of the crutches he had now thrown aside.

Conrad himself was no less anxious than his friend to make this trial; but he did not say much to his grandmother about it, for fear another disappointment should await them. He also wished to avoid all discussion about this visit to Lutterworth; and another topic was now the subject of talk on all sides, so that Wycliffe and his friends might hope to be forgotten and left alone for a time.

For years there had been two rival popes—one reigning and issuing his laws from Rome, the other from Avignon; and these two *infallible* rivals, not content with heaping bulls, curses, and anathemas upon each other, had now come to open war.

INFALLIBLE: *supposedly unable to make an error*
BULLS: *proclamations*
ANATHEMAS: *divine judgments*

The Pontiff of Rome had promulgated a crusade against the Pontiff of Avignon, and England was to be foremost in the strife. The Bishop of Norwich was to be at the head of the English host; and the same indulgences were to be granted as to the crusaders in the Holy Land.

Every town and every village was beginning to be in a ferment of fear, expectancy, and restless excitement, for the Archbishop of Canterbury had issued orders that in every church prayers should be offered for the success of the expedition, and the people urged to give; or, if not willing to give, money, jewels, property of all descriptions, should be extorted from them upon any pretense that was at all plausible, in order to meet the expenses of the undertaking.

As Conrad was on his way to Lutterworth his litter was stopped by a crowd of 'prentice lads from the town and farm laborers, who were gathered round a monk, listening to his fierce denunciations of the Avignon pope, who was charged with being the cause of heavy taxes being levied, and every oppression that the world groaned under.

Then the crowd were exhorted to take up arms instantly, and be led by that brave captain of the Lord, the Bishop of Norwich, who had already proved his martial courage, and would lead them on from victory to victory, until every town in wealthy Flanders had yielded such an amount of spoil that the conquerors would come home laden with riches.

PROMULGATED: *declared*
INDULGENCES: *forgivenesses for sins*
MARTIAL: *military*

Their superstition, fanaticism, ambition, and cupidity, being thus appealed to, little wonder was it that the ignorant crowd were ready to do anything that the monk might bid them, or that they went beyond his orders, and tried to drag off any who were still unwilling to join the crusading host.

The litter had stopped, for the roadway was completely blocked up; and just as the monk had finished speaking the crowd caught sight of Conrad, and the next minute, amid fierce cries of, "Join the holy war! join the new crusade!" Conrad was dragged from his carriage and thrown upon the ground. How much further the mob might have gone in their wild folly it is hard to say, but at this moment one of those who had been sent to fetch Conrad rushed forward to his rescue.

"Are ye all mad or blind, that ye cannot see that he is but a boy, and lame to boot?" cried the man, raising Conrad as he spoke.

The boy, though somewhat shaken, was not frightened. "They did not know I was lame," he said, glancing at his poor shrunken legs; and the crowd, now seeing the mistake they had made, fell back, somewhat ashamed.

"And so ye would have me join your holy war—the new crusade of one pope against the other! Is this the reformation the world is groaning for?"

But the crowd were too excited and impatient to listen to a poor lame boy, who could be of no possible use in the world; and so they rushed after the monk, while Conrad was lifted into the litter

CUPIDITY: *greed*

again, and carried on toward Lutterworth.

Before the town was reached there was another hindrance, for near a stone cross by the roadside stood a poor scholar—one who had learned the truth of God from the lips of Wycliffe at Oxford, and was now traveling through the length and breadth of the land, proclaiming the glorious Gospel of the grace of God.

Conrad would have liked to stay and listen to the preacher; but the men who had been sent to fetch him were anxious to reach Lutterworth before sunset, and when they got there it was easy to understand their anxiety about this. All the town seemed to have gone crazy. Fathers were searching and inquiring for missing sons, and masters for their 'prentice lads, most of whom had run off in the course of the day to hear the monk's sermon about the crusade, and had not returned.

When the hostelry was reached where Sir John Oldcastle and his friends were staying, they found the house, like the town, in a state of great confusion. Turnspits and ostlers, as well as stablemen, waiters, and drawers, had alike run off, and the guests were calling for supper and for their horses to be tended, while the host was at his wits' end to know what to do with his impatient customers.

"Thou art like to go supperless to bed tonight, Conrad," said Sir John, with something of a gloomy smile, as the boy was carried into the room.

"Nay, nay; we will wait yet a little while; and if supper be not served I will ask mine host to let me

TURNSPITS: *servants who turn spits of roasting meat*
OSTLERS: *servants who tend horses at an inn*

cook it," said the scholar, who sat writing near the window.

"Thou shalt be cook, and I will be thy turnspit," said Sir John, laughing. "I had rather things were so than that there should be no supper for Master Jerome when he cometh. Thou wilt see thy kinsman tonight, Conrad," he added, "for he hath promised to spend some hours with us."

Conrad cared far more for this than for the best-served supper that could be spread; for he had made up his mind to ask some questions that his mother and grandmother alike refused to answer. He had not to wait long before their visitor was announced, and with almost trembling impatience and earnestness Conrad leaned forward to look at the grave, gentle-looking young man, as he entered the room. A warm friendship seemed to have sprung up already between Sir John and Jerome, and there they stood, England and Bohemia's future martyrs, clasping each other's hands with the warmth of a fraternal embrace.

"Now I will present thee to a countryman and kinsman of thine own, Master Jerome. Little Conrad here is from Prague, and his grandam saith is of kin to thee."

"Thou dost know me?" said Jerome, questioningly.

"Nay, my grandam said thou wert of kin to our family," answered Conrad; "but thou hadst left Prague before we came with the Princess Anne to England."

DRAWERS: *servants who serve drinks*
FRATERNAL: *brotherly*

"And what is thy name?" asked the Bohemian.

"My grandam's name is Ursula von Zitka; but I know not what mine is, except Conrad."

"Is thy mother's name Ermengarde?" asked Jerome.

"Yes, and she is in the service of the Princess Anne," said Conrad.

"And married an Englishman?" continued Faulfisch.

Conrad shook his head. "I know naught concerning my father; my grandam would never tell me even his name."

"Then he is dead, I ween," said Jerome.

"Nay, I know not even that. I asked my mother once, but it was so sore a grief to her even to hear it mentioned that I have not done so since."

"And thou dost not know his name, or whether he be alive or dead!" uttered Jerome.

"Nay, I know naught; but I prithee tell me all thou knowest, for that my grandam is hiding something from me—some mystery—some shame with which my father is connected—I am certainly assured."

"Mystery—shame! Who dareth to say that Edward Trueman hath aught to do with either?" exclaimed Faulfisch.

"Was my father's name Trueman?" interrupted Conrad, eagerly.

"Ah, my little knave, if thou art Ermengarde von Zitka's son, Edward Trueman was thy father; and right worthy was he of the name, for he was true to God and man, I trow."

Conrad was puzzled, and knew not what to say. From hints and words that he had sometimes heard passing between his mother and grandmother, he had for some time suspected that his father was an Englishman. He also recollected that when his mother first brought old Ned Trueman home with her, on the day his grandmother had started for Canterbury, she had seemed uneasy and anxious; and, also, when Dame Ursula came back, and heard the old man's name mentioned, she seemed uncomfortable, and asked him many questions about the mason—where he lived, whether he had ever been beyond the seas, and whether he had any children. He had thought at the time that it was her intense hatred of Lollardism that prompted all these questions; and he himself never knew that the old man had a son until he heard his brother Martin's tale. Could it be that this lost son was his father?

His next question was even more eager in its intense earnestness. "Where is my father now?" he asked.

But Jerome could only shake his head.

"He must be dead, my poor little knave, or he would be with thee in England, I trow," he said sadly.

"Didst thou see him die?" asked Conrad.

"Nay, my little knave, I had left Prague before thou wast born."

"And thou hast not heard from others that he was dead?"

"Nay."

"Then he is not dead; my father is still alive, and I will find him!" said Conrad, excitedly.

Sir John Oldcastle looked at the usually pale face, now flushed with excitement, and then at the Bohemian scholar, so grave and calm, in his surprise at the boy's words; but when Jerome would have spoken again the young nobleman interrupted him.

"Do not contradict the little knave!" he said; "thou dost not know Conrad yet; wait awhile, and talk of this matter again when thou art better acquainted; and meanwhile tell us how it fareth with godly Master Wycliffe, for thou hast seen him today, I trow?"

"Yes, I left him but an hour since; and he purposeth to preach on this new crusade on the morrow."

"Then thou shalt go and hear him, Conrad," said Sir John. "What said he concerning the Avignon pope?" he asked, turning to Jerome once more.

"He hopeth that these two Antichrists, who are now cursing each other so bitterly, may help to bring a blessing on the world."

"The popes bring a blessing!" uttered the poor scholar, in amazement.

"Not of their own will, I trow; they would fain keep the world in darkness and ignorance even to the end; but men are beginning to find it is dark, and to grope for the light. They are crying for liberty; they are striving to break the bonds in which they have so long been held, and now, with the two popes each issuing laws, they will learn to see that these are but evil priests seeking their own glory and power. He hopeth, too, that the nations will call for a council to sit and judge this schism in the Church, and that the people's cry for a reformation may be heard then, and evils that have long needed amendment may be amended."

"What sayest thou?" asked Sir John Oldcastle, turning to the poor scholar.

"I greatly fear that no council will amend such sore evils as these under which the Church now groaneth," he said.

"But if Master Wycliffe saith—"

"Nay, nay; thou knowest that Master Wycliffe would not have men think as he saith, but he would fain teach them to think for themselves an' they can; and so I deem it no dishonor to Master Wycliffe that I see not as he seeth in this matter."

"'Tis not so much what he seeth as what he hopeth from this council," said Jerome.

"*We* have little to hope from a council, I trow—we shall be adjudged as vile heretics!" said the scholar.

"Nay, nay; if a council of the Church were called to reform its abuses, it would be seen that the doctrine Master Wycliffe doth teach is not heresy, but

SCHISM: *division*

the very truth of God," said Sir John. "I am not to be a learned doctor, but a soldier; but there are many wise and learned men who would be called to a council, that think as I do this day."

Conrad paid but little heed to this talk of a council of the Church now, for his mind was too full of thought concerning his unknown father; and he longed to question Master Jerome further about this matter.

Sir John Oldcastle knew what was in his mind, and so, after the long-delayed supper had been served, he and his friend, the scholar, betook themselves to a distant recess, to talk over their plans, leaving Conrad and his kinsman to talk of their family affairs without interruption.

There were questions and cross-questions, Conrad telling out plainly all his suspicions and fears concerning his father's fate—all he had ever heard from his grandmother, her evident aversion to the topic, and how she had said that heresy such as Dr. Wycliffe's had cursed his childhood, and made him a helpless cripple, as well as herself and his mother miserable and disgraced.

"Disgraced!" repeated Jerome; and then he became deeply engrossed in thought.

Conrad would not disturb him for some time, but at length he said, "Thou didst know my father?"

"Yes, I knew him, Conrad; and when I return to Bohemia I will make inquiries for him among others of our friends. Didst thou ever hear of Conrad Strickna and Matthias Janovius? They were accounted heretics by many. Janovius, who was confessor to the Emperor Charles, the father of Queen Anne, begged that he would call a general council for the reformation of the Church; but for this, and his defense of the people receiving the sacrament in both kinds, and also for preaching plainly against the abuses of the Church and clergy, he was banished from Bohemia by the command of the pope. Did thy mother ever tell thee of the troubles that fell upon many families in Prague?"

Conrad shook his head. "I have heard my grandam say that there were heretics in Bohemia."

"But she did not tell thee thy father was one of these?"

"Nay; but I—I feared it," said Conrad.

"Nay, thy father's son should glory in it!" said Jerome, warmly.

"I cannot even be glad yet; but I will seek my father; it shall be my life-work to find him, or know how he died," said Conrad, as their friends once more joined them.

Chapter XII

The Death of Wycliffe

THE good folk of Lutterworth were much perplexed and very angry at the hasty departure of so many of their young men, but they were in less of a dilemma than many other towns in the kingdom; for this new crusade to help one pontiff against the other served the double purpose of drawing men's minds away from the subject of a reform being needed in the Church, and also strengthened the hold of the Church more firmly upon the people. In Lutterworth the doctrines of Dr. Wycliffe had been working like unseen leaven for some time, and so this wild crusade of the warlike prelate, the Bishop of Norwich, was in rather ill odor among all but the young and inexperienced, who were easily led away by the mere excitement of the scheme, and the hope of speedily acquiring wealth, as well as of seeing new and strange countries.

Dr. Wycliffe was not less earnest than his enemies, the monks, in turning this business to

LEAVEN: *yeast*
IN RATHER ILL ODOR: *unpopular*

account; and the day after Conrad arrived a sermon was announced to be preached at the market cross on this new crusade. That Dr. Wycliffe denounced it most unsparingly is easy to imagine; but Conrad was hardly prepared to hear him say that for men to trust to such works as these was wholly in vain; still less was he prepared to hear the next words, uttered in a deeply earnest but persuasive tone of voice, "Trust wholly to Christ; rely altogether upon His sufferings, and seek not to be justified in any other way than by His righteousness."

Then Wycliffe went on to speak of the worship and invocation of saints, that being a festival of the Church; and he said, "The festival of the day is to no purpose, if it does not tend to magnify Jesus Christ, and induce men to love Him. Moreover, our Redeemer, Jesus Christ, is very God as well as very man; and therefore, on account of His Divinity, He must infinitely exceed any other man. And this consideration induces many to think that it would be expedient to worship no other being among men except Jesus Christ, inasmuch as He is the best Mediator and best Intercessor; and they likewise think that when this was the practice of the Church it increased and prospered much better than it doth now. What folly, then, to apply to any other person to be our intercessor! What folly to choose of two persons proposed the less eligible of the two to be our intercessor! Would anyone choose the king's buffoon to be an

INVOCATION OF SAINTS: *praying to saints for help*
BUFFOON: *court jester*

intercessor? The saints in heaven, indeed, are not buffoons, but in dignity they are less, compared with Jesus Christ, than a buffoon is, compared with an earthly king."

Conrad sat and watched the keen, penetrating gaze, the deep, earnest eyes, of Dr. Wycliffe, almost fascinated by the strange words. They were not altogether strange, either, for Margery had spoken some such words before; but then it was in the privacy of his room. But to hear such things publicly taught, and by one accounted learned, even by his enemies—one, too, who belonged himself to that mystically holy body, the clergy, was something so new and startling that long after the crowd had begun to disperse, Conrad still leaned back in his litter, gazing at the grand old man who wielded such a mighty power in England.

As soon as the space round the preacher was somewhat cleared, Sir John Oldcastle and Jerome Faulfisch pressed forward to speak to him. He greeted the two friends warmly, and as he passed near the litter he paused and spoke a few words to Conrad—words that won the boy's heart at once. "Thou wouldst be brave, and do a man's work in the world; in any case, my little knave, pray that thou mayest be brave, and do God's work."

Conrad bowed his head. "Wilt thou pray for me, worshipful sir?" he murmured.

"Ah, that will I; and this thy friend, Jerome of Prague, will do the same, for thou art of kin to him, and may help him in his heart's desire, the carrying of the Gospel to his beloved Bohemia."

"I must seek my father first, and then—" but before he could finish someone else came to claim the priest's attention.

To try walking about with the crutches Sir John Oldcastle had prepared for him, was something of a diversion for Conrad, and prevented him from thinking uninterruptedly of what he had determined should be his life's work. He would fain have set off to Bohemia at once, if it had been practicable; but Master Faulfisch soon convinced him that such a journey was impossible at present, and that he would be much more likely to succeed in his quest by-and-by if he remained at Lutterworth for the present, and studied in the school that had been opened by one of Dr. Wycliffe's poor scholars. Master Jerome promised the boy that his first work, after he got back to Prague, should be to discover his old friend, and that he would see his mother before he left England, and find out all she knew about the matter.

This contented Conrad; nay, he was more than content when Faulfisch promised to send a letter for him whenever he could find a trusty messenger that would bring letters to Dr. Wycliffe. After a few trials he was able to move about a little with the crutches; but his progress was very slow, for his back, as well as his limbs, were weak. Still, slow as it was, Conrad was delighted at the novelty of being able to walk even a few steps; and when he heard that one of Dr. Wycliffe's poor scholars thought he might gain strength by being in the open air more, and by using a certain decoction of salt and water in which some costly stones had been laid, he resolved to try this remedy.

It was very seldom that Conrad had been able to go out; but now that he could walk he determined to use his crutches, even though he could only get outside the door at first and sit upon the ground. He made up his mind that he would not leave Lutterworth, if he could help it; but whether his grandmother could be persuaded to come and live in the town, especially when she knew that the school he wished to attend was under the direction of Dr. Wycliffe, he did not know. Happily, this difficulty was settled for him by old Martin, his host, who came to the hostelry, after he had been there about a week, to say that he was obliged to move into the town, for his son, who helped him in his garden, and brought the supplies they needed from the town, had joined this new crusade, greatly to the grief and perplexity of his father and mother, who were growing more feeble every month.

"Ye see, worshipful sirs, we shall be starved of a certain if we abide where we are; for when winter comes the roads are so bad that my poor old limbs cannot move for sticking in the mire. I would fain move into the town, too, that my dame may go to church sometimes, and hear the wondrous good

DECOCTION: *an extract obtained by boiling down*

words of Master Wycliffe, for they have been a marvelous comfort to me. Not that I have not heard something of the like before; my master, the great Duke of Lancaster, bade us ever help the poor scholars who were traveling through the country teaching men the good words they had learned from Dr. Wycliffe; and so I have often heard them preach in the great hall of the Savoy Palace, at London, before the rebels burned it."

The old man would have gone on to tell how many goodly houses in London the rebels had burned and sacked besides his master's, had he not been interrupted by Sir John Oldcastle, who was almost as eager about Conrad staying at Lutterworth as the boy himself.

"Then thou art coming to live at Lutterworth, Martin, and would fain have this little knave and his grandam live with thee still?"

"An it please them, I should, for they were commended to me by my lord duke himself."

"But what saith my grandam, Master Martin?" asked Conrad.

"The dame will be pleased to come an it pleaseth thee," replied Martin; "but she feared that when thy friends left the town thou mightest pine for the fields and hedges again, as thou lovest them so much; for me, I like a town now, and thy grandam is something of my mind, I trow."

"Then, if Dame Ursula is pleased to come, the matter is settled, for Conrad will be pleased to stay," said Sir John, quickly; and, having ordered some refreshment to be brought for the old man, he went out.

While Martin was regaling himself with slices of boar's head and brawn, and washing it down with copious draughts of strong ale, Conrad questioned him about his brother in London, old Ned Trueman, and how long his son had been away. He did not tell him of his own supposed relationship to himself, for his friends had advised that this should be kept a secret at present, more especially as Dame Ursula so bitterly hated all heretics.

But old Martin either had known very little about his nephew, or had, during the lapse of years, forgotten almost all he had known, beyond the bare fact that young Ned had gone beyond the seas; of his father being deeply grieved at his loss he knew nothing. It was arranged now that Conrad should at once commence his studies at the school, and remain in Lutterworth until his grandmother could join him.

For a few weeks longer he had the pleasant company of Sir John Oldcastle, who, scarcely more than a boy himself, could enter most enthusiastically into all Conrad's plans for the future. A clever scholar himself, he could sympathize with Conrad's desire to be a "seraphic doctor;" while Conrad had the greatest admiration for the career Sir John had marked out for himself—that of a soldier. To fight the hereditary foes of his country, the

REGALING: *feasting*
BRAWN: *pickled boar*
COPIOUS DRAUGHTS: *numerous drinks*

French; to lead men on from victory to victory, and teach the victors how to be merciful and compassionate to their conquered enemies, by respecting the rights of property wherever it was possible, and raising an arm in defense of helpless women and children, instead of ruthlessly murdering, thus robbing war of half its horrors—this was the young knight's dream; and he and Conrad would discuss this while his tutor and Jerome of Prague were talking over the merits of Dr. Wycliffe's various works.

The pleasant talks came to an end at last, however, for as soon as old Martin could find a house to suit him he removed to the town. Sir John stayed on until they came, for he greatly feared that Dame Ursula would raise a violent objection to Conrad's attending the school. He had already commenced his studies there, for it had been thought advisable that this should be done before the old lady came, although they feared it would not make much difference in the opposition she would be sure to entertain.

But, strange to say, she paid very little heed to this when Conrad told her. She was so overjoyed to see him slowly limp across the room on his crutches, and so delighted at the idea of preparing the salt-and-water decoction, in which a precious stone from a serpent's head was to be soaked every day, that she had no thought for anything else.

"'Tis the wonderful stone in which the strength lies, and I will take care 'tis well-soaked, Conrad," she said; and the boy was glad that his grandmother could still do something for him, for that her life was bound up in him he knew.

There was certainly a change in Dame Ursula this summer, and Conrad was not the only one who noticed it. She seemed suddenly to have grown feeble where she was so energetic and fierce before. Heresy seemed to have lost all its horror, and she would calmly listen to old Martin repeating what he could remember of Dr. Wycliffe's last sermon. Conrad sometimes feared her mind must be failing when he heard this, and recollected how the very name of Wycliffe had been sufficient to put her into a violent passion. He could scarcely hope that there was any change in her own religious opinions, for she never entered Lutterworth Church, but went sometimes to hear a monk recite the legend of some saint, and chose for her confessor one who was known to be the bitter enemy of Dr. Wycliffe. Conrad was truly thankful for such unwonted peace; and yet it made him strangely anxious about his grandmother. All through the summer and autumn of that year, 1384, he watched her with the deepest solicitude, and every hour not spent at school was passed with her.

There was another, too, in Lutterworth, whose failing health and untiring mental exertions were a source of great anxiety to anxious friends. Never since had Dr. Wycliffe preached at the market cross, and it was seldom now that he could stand

SOLICITUDE: *attentiveness*

TRANSUBSTANTIATION: *the belief that the bread and wine used in communion become the physical body of Christ* up in the pulpit of his own parish church. Paralysis had seized him some time before; and, although it was hoped he might be spared many years longer, his untiring efforts in his study, and the number of tracts and pamphlets that came from his pen to be copied and sent broadcast over England, almost forbade the hope.

Conrad had read many of these now, and was learning to copy them in English, and for his own amusement translated them into Bohemian. He thought it would please his friend, Master Jerome Faulfisch, to receive one of these pamphlets translated into their native language, and so he was most diligent and careful in this self-imposed task.

He had learned by this time that Dr. Wycliffe differed from the Church in other matters besides the doctrine of transubstantiation. To auricular confession, the sale of indulgences, the invocation of saints, the worship of images, prayers for the dead, and the celibacy of the clergy, he was decidedly opposed; and in language that the poorest and most unlearned could understand, he denounced them in all his English tracts. The more learned books were written in Latin, for the use of his scholars, who, he hoped, would carry on his work when he was gone.

That the time of his departure was so near, was little guessed; but as the winter drew on it became evident that Dr. Wycliffe would feel it severely. Toward the end of December, however, he seemed

AURICULAR CONFESSION: *private confession of sins to a priest*

CELIBACY: *remaining unmarried*

stronger for a day or two, and he decided to conduct the service in church himself on the twenty-ninth of that month. It was the festival of some saint; and the news that Dr. Wycliffe himself would preach brought many that winter's day.

Old Martin and Conrad were among the first comers, for a commodious corner where the lame boy could recline had been found for him near the altar; and, as a crowd might be expected, they were anxious to get there in good time.

Conrad noticed a change in the eager, penetrating countenance of Dr. Wycliffe, and there was an ashen greyness in it; but still he seemed to be in moderate health, and began to read the service of the mass in a clear voice. But just as he was about to elevate the host his voice suddenly failed, the consecrated bread fell from his hand, and he fell prostrate on the steps of the altar. Eager, loving hands raised him, but he was speechless and insensible. It was a second attack of paralysis; and two days after he died, to the intense grief of hundreds of friends, and the deep joy of as many enemies, who, now that his voice was silenced by death, hoped that the troublesome doctrines he taught might die also.

Wycliffe's Pulpit

COMMODIOUS: *spacious*
PROSTRATE: *laid out flat*
INSENSIBLE: *unconscious*

Chapter XIII

Will the Truth Die?

THE death of Dr. Wycliffe was felt as a severe blow, and many feared that the new doctrines he had taught—new to that and many previous ages, but older in truth than the ceremonies and corruptions beneath which they had been long buried—would soon be forgotten.

Poor old Martin, from being one of the most sanguine believers in a reformation being near at hand, now lost all hope, and often poured out his lamentations to Conrad about it. "Ah, my little knave, I thought to see it in my day—this reformation that all men are talking of. I thought that my master, the great duke, and Dr. Wycliffe together, would do this for England, at least; but now that godly Master Wycliffe hath been taken, I fear me 'tis an end of all hope."

"Nay, nay; say not so, Master Martin; for the new teaching of Dr. Wycliffe, being the truth of God, cannot die; and too many have learned to love the truth to let it be forgotten."

SANGUINE: *confident*

But old Martin shook his head sadly. "Thou dost not know the world, Conrad. I tell thee this, that those who persecuted Dr. Wycliffe, and drove him from Oxford, will persecute those who hold his doctrine, and drive them from the world, if it be possible."

"But they will not kill the truth, Martin," said Conrad, calmly. "I heard one of the poor priests who came into the school today telling of this very matter, and it hath greatly cheered me. 'The spring will be coming anon,' he said; 'and thou wilt see these bare trees clothed with leaves, and thou wilt call them new leaves, and so they are; but the like leaves had budded and blossomed on the trees afore-time. And so it is, I ween, with these truths—these new doctrines taught by Dr. Wycliffe: they are the old, old truths that were taught by the Lord Jesus Christ and His apostles and the early martyrs of the Church; but as the Church grew worldly, and proud, and self-seeking, these truths became buried and forgotten, except as they lived in the hearts of a few of God's chosen people. But though buried deep beneath worldliness and pride, and ambition and corruption, they were not dead, for the truth can never die; and now, at the breath of God, by the voice of Dr. Wycliffe, they are once more seen peeping forth from the cerements in which the Church had bound them.'"

"And thinkest thou the Church will be pulled to pieces quietly, that the truth may blossom in the world again?" asked old Martin, angrily.

CEREMENTS: *graveclothes*

"If 'tis a true Church, and knoweth the times and seasons, and this breath of God's mouth that is rushing through the world creating a new spring in men's hearts and lives; and if not—"

"It will not, I tell thee, Conrad. Thou art but a lad, and knowest not the ways of great prelates, as I have seen them. Thinkest thou they will give up their wealth, and live sober, godly lives, teaching and preaching like a poor priest? Dost thou think the monks and friars will give up a life of luxury and idleness, and work like a poor villein, instead of being ignorant and lazy, that they may teach like any poor scholar? Nay, nay, Conrad; Dr. Wycliffe hath begun to pull down the hornets' nests, and hath made havoc of many fair-seeming things in the Church; but the hornets will abide in their nests still; and no better things being found for those that are destroyed, men will cling to them still, and the Church will laugh to scorn twenty Dr. Wycliffes, I trow."

"Nay, but if this be God's time for giving to the world a reformer and a reformation," said Conrad, "then—"

"But what if the world will none of it?" interrupted Martin.

"Nay, but the world is crying and groaning for it," said Conrad, almost as quickly.

"Yea, the world is crying for it, as thou sayest; but is it such a reformation as God would give—as Dr. Wycliffe taught by life and doctrine—that the world would have? I trow not, Conrad, I trow not," said the old man, shaking his head.

"But if it be God's time, Master Martin, the world *must* have it," said Conrad.

The old man sat musing for a minute or two, and then said, "God worketh in the world by means of men, as He doth in the field by sunshine and showers but men are not suns nor raindrops. God worketh by them through their wills; and if they will not to work with Him, then is the work stayed, even though it be God's work, and for the good of men. This I heard from Dr. Wycliffe himself, my little knave."

"But Dr. Wycliffe hoped there would be a reformation in the Church soon," said Conrad, energetically. "He hoped the nations would call a council of the Church to correct its abuses, and—"

"Nay, nay, Conrad; 'tis as useless to talk of councils as of popes. I shall not live to see a reformation, though it may be thou wilt, if thou art spared to a good old age."

The conversation was interrupted here by the entrance of Dame Ursula, to whom the very word "reformation" was a detestation and a horror. She had not mentioned the name of Wycliffe, but it was easy to see that his death was a source of joy to her; and she began to look forward to the time when the little band of his disciples at Lutterworth should be dispersed, and Conrad would return to the Church once more, and believe it perfect and holy, as she herself did.

DETESTATION: *hated thing*

But as the weeks and months went on she saw little sign of her hopes being fulfilled. The school where the reformer's doctrines were taught and his books copied and translated was still carried on, and Conrad was now one of its foremost pupils.

She wished it were otherwise. She almost wished he would don a white cloak, with the red cross on one shoulder, that the 'prentice lads assumed now, in imitation of the old crusaders; for the army in Flanders, with its bishop-leader, was daily being recruited, and the excitement of this "holy war" was by no means at an end. But oh, the tale of horror that came with the news of their first success! They took Gravelines, and they took Dunkerque, hewing men, women, and children to pieces in one vast massacre; and the woes of war were doubled and trebled in this new crusade of Christian against Christian, pope against pope.

But Conrad evinced no desire to join the white-cloaked, red-crossed bands that sometimes paraded through the streets; he did not even express a wish to be able to throw his crutches aside, but seemed quite content to limp backward and forward to school, or for a short ramble occasionally with his grandmother and old Martin.

In a few months came other news from the seat of war in Flanders. Disaster followed disaster, and the bishop-general was at last glad to purchase an inglorious retreat by giving up all the towns he had taken; and the Avignon pope reigned in

EVINCED: *showed*
INGLORIOUS: *disgraceful*

undisturbed luxury, while his rival at Rome cared not a jot for the torrents of human blood that had been spilled in his name.

But after a time other news reached Lutterworth, that affected the little company of Wycliffe's disciples far more deeply. The prelates had waited some three years now, hoping that, Wycliffe being dead, the doctrines he had taught would be forgotten; but, so far from this being the case, they were spreading to so great an extent that in some counties of England complaint was made that every second man was a Lollard. In London the citizens were embracing the new doctrines, and even some of the clergy themselves. One of the pope's chaplains, an Augustinian friar, preached publicly at St. Christopher's Church on the vices of the clergy. His fellow-monks burst into the church, and served him with an interdict; but the Lollards drove them out, and the chaplain soon after affixed a writing on the doors of St. Paul's that he had "escaped from the companionship of the worst of men to the most perfect and holy life of a Lollard." But if this gave joy and hope to many who were still waiting and watching for the dawn of the hoped-for reformation—hoping for someone to appear who could take Dr. Wycliffe's place as the leader, the teacher, the reformer—their joy was but of short duration; for it was soon noised abroad that the Archbishop of Canterbury had determined to put down Lollardism, and was coming

INTERDICT: *a formal order forbidding participation in the services of the church* to Leicester, there to hold a court, and solemnly excommunicate, with bell, book, and candle, all who would not read a public recantation of their errors. Many recanted, of course, and many more were frightened into silence or attending the confessional again; and Archbishop Courtney may have thought he had given a severe check to Lollardism, while many continued praying and watching for the leader to arise who could take Wycliffe's place.

This want of a leader was felt most severely, and led to a good many mistakes on the part of some who called themselves Lollards, but had very little of the true spirit of Wycliffe. Doubtless in those turbulent and unsettled times—turbulent and unsettled even for that age—many things were charged to the Lollards of which they were not guilty; for the dethronement and death of King Richard, and the accession of his cousin, Henry IV, son of the Duke of Lancaster, with other political troubles, almost disorganized every rank in society for some time. Queen Anne had died at the palace of Shene some years before the disastrous close of her husband's reign, and about ten years after the death of Wycliffe; and soon after her death Dame Ermengarde came to Lutterworth, to make arrangements for their speedy return to Bohemia. To her great surprise, Dame Ursula positively refused to go back.

"But, my mother, thou hast often said thou wouldst go back to Prague, for thou likest not this

EXCOMMUNICATE: *banish from the church*
RECANTATION: *formal denial*
ACCESSION: *crowning*

country," said her daughter; and it was evident that she was greatly disappointed by her mother's refusal to return to their native country.

Conrad, too, urged that she would go for his sake, as he greatly longed to see the place where he was born, and the friends who had known his father. But at the mention of his father Dame Ursula seemed more determined than ever not to leave Lutterworth.

Conrad was no longer a child, but a grave, thoughtful young man, and he noticed the change in his grandmother's manner at the mention of his father.

"It is ever so, my mother," he said, when he mentioned this circumstance to her afterwards. Dame Ermengarde tried to avoid this subject now, as she had done before when he had told her of Jerome Faulfisch and what he had said concerning his father. But Conrad would not be put off again. "I know my father was an Englishman—one Edward Trueman, so that my name is of right Conrad Trueman, and not Conrad von Zitka," he said. "Hast thou seen my grandfather of late?" he asked.

"Thy grandfather, Conrad?"

"Yes; the kindly old mason who came so often to see me at Holywell. He knew not that I was the child of his lost son; and I have kept the thing secret too long, I fear, but he shall know it ere long."

"Conrad, what art thou saying?" asked his mother, with whitening lips.

"That I mean to seek for my father until I find him, or learn the manner of his death."

"Conrad, Conrad, thou must not do this—thou must not let the name of Trueman be heard in Prague! Von Zitka is an old, an honored name in Bohemia; be content to bear that, my son, my Conrad!"

But Conrad drew himself away as his mother would have embraced him.

"Thou speakest thus, my mother, and of my father, too? Thou sayest I shall bear my grandam's name; but I have no right to that, since my father's name was Trueman; and this I know from Jerome Faulfisch. He promised to search for him when he went back to Bohemia; but since Dr. Wycliffe died no letter hath come from him, and so, now I am a man, I will begin the work to which I have vowed to devote my life, to—to find my father. Wilt thou help me, my mother?"

"I cannot! Oh, Conrad, I cannot! Would to God that I could!" and Dame Ermengarde fell back unconscious, feebly murmuring the last words.

Chapter XIV

In London

CONRAD was no longer a child, but still he could not return to Bohemia against the wishes of his mother, and he knew she would never consent to his going without her; while to attempt to move his grandmother from her determination not to leave England was equally useless, and so the family stayed on at Lutterworth for some time; but just after the deposition of King Richard the old lady consented to go to London, for Conrad was anxious for many reasons to remove thither. He wanted to see Ned Trueman, and try to discover from him whether the old man was, as he imagined, his grandfather. He blamed himself now for not trying to make sure of this before, for only one letter had reached him from Prague during all these years, and Master Jerome Faulfisch had not been able to discover any clue to his father's fate.

Dame Ermengarde was rather unwilling to go back to London, for Conrad made no secret of being a Lollard; and, as these opinions were growing

DEPOSITION: *removal*

more dangerous every day, she thought he would be safer in quiet, out-of-the-way Lutterworth.

But Conrad thought otherwise. "My mother, more than half the citizens of London are Lollards now, and the new king—this Henry of Lancaster—hath but little right to the crown, and so he will not dare to persecute the Lollards, even if he desire not to follow in his father's steps in being their protector, for 'tis to the people he must look, I trow, if he would conquer his foes and keep his throne."

And so in the spring of the year 1400 the little family traveled by slow stages to London, for Dame Ursula was very feeble now, and the ill-kept roads and the clumsy conveyances made traveling both tedious and fatiguing to those who could not ride on horseback.

Conrad had decided to seek Master Winchester and his old friend Mistress Margery, as soon as his mother and grandmother were settled near their old home in Holywell, and so a day or two after their arrival he set out on this errand.

To find Master Winchester, the merchant of Chepe, was not difficult; but it was less easy for a lame man to push his way between the itinerant vendors of different wares, keep his crutches from slipping in the narrow, filthy streets, and look after his personal belongings, to see that they were not stolen. In this latter particular he was not successful, for he scarcely entered the city before his cap was snatched from his head, and the rogue made off with it so fast that Conrad could not hope to catch him, and so gave up the attempt at once.

Close to Master Winchester's stall, however, he saw the cap again; the very rogue who had stolen it was offering it for sale with several others of different sorts that were, doubtless, obtained in the same way.

Conrad, unused to the ways of London, claimed his cap, and taxed the rogue with the theft; but the man so stoutly maintained his innocence, calling Conrad a seditious Lollard, and gathering a crowd of the roughest of the people around them, that at last, to escape the annoyance, he was glad to buy his cap at its full value, rather than present himself at the merchant's house without one.

Master Winchester recollected the name of Conrad as soon as it was mentioned, and at once invited him to go in and see his niece, while he sent to inform his daughter, Dame Margery Gilpin, of his arrival.

Conrad had forgotten the change that the passing years had made in himself, and almost expected to see the Mistress Margery he had last seen at Holywell; he was not, therefore, at all prepared to see a stout, comely matron, with two rosy well-grown boys at her side, almost as tall as the Mistress Margery of the old days. He felt a little disappointed, he scarcely knew why, at finding

TAXED: *charged*
SEDITIOUS: *rebellious*
COMELY: *attractive*

her—Dame Gilpin, too; while she, recalling her dismissal as his teacher, wondered that he should seek those who were everywhere known as most obstinate Lollards.

Before they had exchanged a dozen words, however, Dame Gilpin knew that her old pupil was as much a Lollard as herself, and so she invited him to go home with her and spend the day at her house. "My father and some other friends among the merchants are to meet at our house about four of the clock, and thou mayest hear how it fareth with us here."

"I shall be right glad to meet any who are friends of thine. But tell me first how fareth it with Master Filpot, the armorer, and his friend Trueman, the mason, and my good friend Master Geoffrey Chaucer."

"Master Filpot is well, and thy friend the mason is as hale as ever; but Master Chaucer is sick, and 'tis greatly feared he will never gain strength again, for he is an old man—seventy-two—and hath seen much travel and many changes. Our good lord, King Henry, hath restored his pension to him, or he would be in sore want, I trow. Hast thou heard of the wondrous poesy he hath writ?"

Conrad shook his head. "We hear but little at Lutterworth," he said.

"Well, he hath writ marvelous tales in poesy of what a certain band of pilgrims did and said on the road to Canterbury. It is not finished yet, for this grievous sickness hath hindered the writing of it, and some fear it will never be finished now."

"I will go and see Master Chaucer before I go to Bohemia," said Conrad.

"Thou art going back to thine own country, then?" said Dame Gilpin.

"I would fain go by the next ship that doth cross the sea, but my grandam is feeble and sick, and, moreover, refuseth to go; so it may be I shall be in London for months or years."

"Then thou must ask Master Chaucer to let thee read his poesy of the Canterbury Tales. 'Twill please thee, I trow, for even Master Wycliffe himself could not show to men the evil lives of monks and priests more plainly than Master Chaucer hath; and 'tis such grand poesy as hath never been writ before, many learned people say."

"Then I will certainly ask Master Chaucer to let me see it," said Conrad; and then he turned to speak to the two boys, while their mother went in search of her father, to tell him she was going to take Conrad home with her.

Master Gilpin was a merchant of Chepe, like his former master and father-in-law, and, like him, was known to be a staunch Lollard.

There were Lollards and Lollards in those days, even as in these there are Christians and Christians. The discontented and seditious—those who made a profit of the disorganized state of the times, and would raise a clamor against all law—these called themselves Lollards. Then there were those who had long sighed for civil liberty, but knew not that they were in bondage to sin while they yielded to their own selfish desires, and often adopted illegal means to obtain redress for their wrongs. These, too, were Lollards. Then last, but not least, was the faithful band of earnest souls who had learned from Dr. Wycliffe not only to be dissatisfied with the teachings and doctrines of the Church of Rome, but also to seek that pardon for the sin which they had learned to feel was a more cruel bondage than the fetters and chains of outward observances which the Church called religion.

Among these last were Dame Gilpin and her husband, and many of their friends were like-minded; but there were others, too, who cared very little for this inner spiritual life, who yet cried most loudly for liberty of conscience, liberty to hold land, and liberty to buy and sell where they pleased; but they cared very little for that liberty wherewith Christ makes His people free, although they called themselves Lollards and devoted followers of Wycliffe.

It seemed that this meeting of the foremost Lollards of London was to discuss what it would be best to do, now that King Henry, to propitiate the Church and its powerful archbishop, Arundel, had declared himself the protector of the Church, and the help of the crown was promised to the clergy in their efforts to put down all itinerant preachers.

PROPITIATE: *make peace with*

"What sayest thou to these things, Master Gilpin?" asked one.

"Thou knowest that I have always advised a quiet, peaceable holding of our own doctrines in the matter of religion; but—"

"Thou knowest Master Gilpin was ever against the writings being set up on every church door and wall in London, threatening that there would be a rising of the Lollards," interrupted another.

"Ah! 'twas an ill-advised act, and hath done much evil, I trow," said Master Winchester.

"Nay, good gossips; but if it hath frightened Archbishop Arundel, and taught him that we cannot be put down, and will not give up striving for our liberties, it is well."

"But hath it done this?" asked two or three together; "or hath it not rather led the king to look upon us as rebels and seditious knaves; and may not our city lose its chartered liberty by it?"

"Nay, nay!" shouted some; but when the clamor had ceased an old man rose to speak whom Conrad had not seen before.

"Our declaration that we be seditious knaves, and ready to rebel against our good lord, hath not frightened the archbishop; but it hath frightened the king and the parliament, and they are going to make a new law, whereby it shall be lawful to burn all heretics condemned by the Church."

For a few minutes the little company could only look at the speaker aghast, and then at each other

VERILY: *truly*

in blank amazement. But that the speaker was one who could not be contradicted in such matters, inasmuch as he was in a position to know what was doing in the court and parliament, they would have been ready to say that such news could not be true.

At last Master Gilpin said, "If it be as thou sayest, then must we look to God to be our helper in the hour of trial!"

"Yea, for we shall verily need help," said Master Sawtree. This man had formerly been a priest at King's Lynn, but, being convicted before the warlike Bishop of Norwich of holding Wycliffe's doctrines, he had been driven out of the diocese, and was now a preacher at St. Osyth, in the City of London.

Everyone looked for Master Sawtree to advise them in this difficulty; but it seemed that he could say nothing beyond exhorting them to study more diligently than ever the Word of God, and to be much in prayer for strength to meet the fiery trial, if it became the duty of any of them to confess Christ before the world. The pale, gentle face of the speaker, and his tremulous, diffident manner, made more impression upon his hearers than the words themselves. Could it have been that he had a premonition of his own weakness in the hour of trial—of his shameful defeat, that yet ended in a glorious victory—for William Sawtree was the protomartyr of the Reformation in England—a

DIFFIDENT: *timid*
PREMONITION: *forewarning*
PROTOMARTYR: *first martyr*

weak and feeble leader of a glorious band of men and women, England's contingent to the "noble army of martyrs," gathered from all ages and all lands?

The announcement that the king and parliament alike contemplated the passing of a law for the burning of heretics, and that this was specially aimed at the Lollards, cast a gloom over the little company; and before they parted that night they had settled that, though they would not give up the purer faith they had learned from Wycliffe, it would be wise to hold their meetings more secretly, and to hide the Bible and books of Wycliffe.

It was a bitter disappointment to Conrad, as well as many others, to find that the son of the Duke of Lancaster, who had been called the "Father of the Reformation," should now forsake that cause, and range himself as its persecutor; but the reason was not far to seek. Henry's title to the throne was one of might against right; and although, to secure the favor of the people, he was daily granting more power to the Commons than any of his predecessors had done, there was another power to be conciliated, greater even than the people at large—the Church. To offend the powerful hierarchy of Rome was to have himself proclaimed as a usurper, his people stirred up to rebel against him, and foreign foes incited to invade the land; and Henry IV loved power and a throne in this world rather than to "share affliction with the

HIS PREDECESSORS: *those who held the position before him*
BE CONCILIATED: *gain the favor of*
USURPER: *someone who has wrongfully seized his position*

people of God"[1] for a little while, and afterward to inherit a kingdom "not made with hands, eternal in the heavens."[2]

The news that had first reached the little company at Dame Gilpin's was speedily confirmed; and when Conrad went to see Master Filpot, the armorer, he found him in such distress as to be scarcely able to work. His business as an armorer had greatly increased of late, and there were now so many new fashions in armor that he was obliged to keep several men employed about the smithy; but when he heard who Conrad was, and the business he had come upon, he motioned him to keep silence until they were out of hearing.

"They are all Lollards, or call themselves such," said Master Filpot, when he had taken his visitor into the house and closed the door; "every second man is a Lollard now, as thou knowest; but there will not be one in ten bold enough to call himself by that name ere long, for there will be a sifting, I trow—a sifting of the wheat from the chaff—and thou knowest what will follow, Conrad."

Conrad shook his head.

Master Filpot leaned forward, and spoke in a low, impressive voice, "The chaff will be scattered, but the wheat will be garnered—garnered up there;" and he pointed upward.

"Nay, Master Filpot, though it be that we are living in evil times, the Church will but try to frighten us, I trow, with this new statute for the burning of

[1] Hebrews 11:25 [2] II Corinthians 5:1

GARNERED: *gathered*

such as conform not to her laws. But I came not to talk about this, but about thine old gossip, Master Trueman. How fareth it with him?"

But before the question could be answered Ned Trueman, with the familiarity of an old friend, had pushed open the door and walked in. He would have retreated when he saw a stranger in the room; but Conrad limped over on his crutches, and seized the old man's hand, for, unlike Dame Gilpin and Master Filpot, Trueman did not look a day older than when he had last seen him.

The mason laughed when Conrad said this. "Ah, my knave, it may be I am not so old as thou deemest me," he said; "the years came on me all at once, and there's no room for more then, I trow. But now tell me what hath brought thee to London? Art thou a Lollard, like the rest of us?"

"Art thou a Lollard?" asked Conrad.

"Nay, how could I help it, loving liberty as I do? Liberty and Lollardism have become one; and I will abide a Lollard and a heretic now," said Trueman, stoutly.

Chapter XV

A Confession

CONRAD thought it would be better to see Trueman alone, to talk over what he had heard from Faulfisch; and so he proposed to pay him a visit the following day, a proposal that quite delighted the old man, although he had no idea what the business could be that Conrad desired to see him about.

"Thou didst have a son who left thee many years since; canst thou tell me anything concerning him?" said Conrad, entering at once upon the business when he saw Trueman the next day.

The old man stared, and his lip quivered as he slowly shook his head. "There is little enough to tell, Master Conrad," he said, sadly. "I thought the knave willful then; but I was too severe, I trow, and Ned never knew how much I loved him. But wherefore didst thou think of this?" he asked.

"I would fain know all thou canst tell me. What manner of man was my father? and—"

"Thy father!" repeated Trueman, staring at Conrad, and then the old man drew his hand across his eyes, as if they were deceiving him.

"Yes, I verily believe thy lost son was my father," said Conrad, in a voice trembling with agitation; and then he told him all he had heard from Jerome of Prague concerning his unknown parent.

"It must be as thou sayest; and, now I look at thee, thou art like my Ned, only that he was a strong, stalwart fellow, fit to fight in any war when he went to Flanders."

"He went to Flanders?" repeated Conrad.

"Ah, whither would he go but there? 'Tis across sea, I trow; and Bohemia is across sea, too, so that 'tis all one after all."

"Wilt thou come and see my mother? It may be she can tell thee whether my father came from Flanders to Bohemia," said Conrad.

"An it be as thou thinkest, I must away to this far country to seek for my son," said Trueman. "And thou, Conrad, thou art his son!"

"I will go with thee, doubt not;" and he fell upon the old man's neck, while Trueman clasped him in his arms in a long embrace.

"My son, my long lost Ned!" he murmured, through his falling tears; and then he looked into Conrad's face again, as if to trace the lineaments of the son he had not seen for so many years. "You are my Ned's child. I can see him in thy face, Conrad—fool that I was not to see it before! but my heart saw it, though my eyes were blinded. And now let us go to thy mother. I must see my Ned's

LINEAMENTS: *features*

wife, my daughter, and ask her to tell me all she knoweth of him."

"She will tell all she can, fear not; but 'tis my grandam that could tell us most, I ween," said Conrad.

"Then she shall tell! I will wring this mystery, this secret, from her!" and the old man clenched his fist, as though he would strike as well as threaten her, if she refused to tell him all she knew.

Dame Ermengarde knew the errand upon which Conrad had gone to see his old friend, and, therefore, was not surprised to see him returning with Conrad; but she was not prepared for such a demonstration of affection, for the old man caught her in his arms, and kissed her as he had kissed Conrad. "Thou wert kind to him—my son—whom I had driven away by my harshness!" he said, as he released her.

Dame Ermengarde was too much overcome to reply for a minute or two, but at length she managed to say, "I—I fear I have not been a good wife to my poor Edward! but—"

"Never mind the past; only tell me where he is—where I can find him—what hath become of him."

But Dame Ermengarde, choked with sobs and almost blinded with tears, could only shake her head as she fell back upon her seat.

"But Dame Ursula knoweth, and she must tell me," said Trueman, firmly.

Dame Ermengarde could only shake her head, and protest that she dare not ask her mother such a question now; but Ned Trueman, hearing the old lady call her daughter, cut short these protestations by going himself to her bedside.

"Dame Ursula, I want my son, and thou shalt tell me where they took him when they carried him away from wife and child!"

The old woman stared at him for a minute or two, and then broke out into a piteous wail. "I knew it! I knew thou wouldst come to wring my secret from me; but I tell thee thou shalt not spoil the good work I have done. If Conrad there is a heretic Lollard, I have saved his father, I trow. The monks have brought him back to the true faith, and he is reconciled to the Church, and a holy monk himself, or he would have come to England long ere this."

"Where is he, woman? What prison didst thou send him to?" cried Trueman, trembling with passion.

Conrad, who had followed his grandfather into the room, saw that little good, but much harm, might be done by this rashness; and so, gently pushing him aside, he said, "Grandam, this is my father's father, and we would fain know what monastery he went to when he went away from Prague."

"Who says I betrayed him to the monks?" demanded the old woman, fiercely; then, changing her tone, she wailed forth, "I could not help it,

"Who says I betrayed him?"

Conrad! I could not help it! The disgrace of having a heretic in my family was so great; and then it was a good work—surely it was a good work. The holy Father Matthias, my confessor, said it would be accounted so good a work that I should escape the pains of purgatory myself, and secure the salvation of thy father and mother, and thine, too; and that thy father should come home again as soon as he was reconciled to the Church. The holy fathers of the Dominican monastery had undertaken to secure his salvation; and so surely I ought to help in so good a work."

Conrad had let her ramble on, hoping that in her present feeble state she would disclose the closely guarded secret; and, now that she had done so, he trembled with excitement, while Trueman was in such a rage as he listened to her that Conrad could with difficulty keep him from seizing and shaking her. At last he got him away from the bedside, and out of the room.

"Thou wilt spoil all by thy rashness!" he said, half-angrily. "Stay here awhile; and doubtless I shall now find where this Dominican monastery is;" and, fearing lest his grandmother's mind should wander again, as it frequently had of late, he went back at once to her bedside.

"Now, Grandam, thou wilt tell me more about thy confessor, and this work that he set thee to do."

"'Twas a good work, Conrad, and the saints will reward me and thy mother for all we have suffered

PURGATORY: *a supposed place of punishment where the dead pay for their sins before going to heaven* in doing it. She thinks I know naught of the suffering; but ah! she knows not that of late I can think of nothing else but the iron-stanchioned door near the gate of the city—"

"What city was it, Grandam?" questioned Conrad.

"What city should it be but Prague? My Ermengarde and all our friends were told that he had left the city—left it on urgent business; and he thought it was so himself until they dragged him into the monastery gates."

"Didst thou see him taken? wert thou with them, Grandam?"

"Was I not with him?" asked Dame Ursula, fiercely. "Thou knowest that my confessor bade me walk with him beyond the city gates three days after thou wert born; and I went. Who said I betrayed him? Who said he turned his pale face toward me, and looked as though I had murdered him? 'Twas a good work, I tell thee; the Church of Bohemia was threatened with overthrow if the heresy was not cast out of her, and our name—our ancient, honorable name—was disgraced by the heresy; and so it surely was a good work to take away the disgrace, and to prove that we were still faithful servants of Holy Church, and that this Englishman was no true von Zitka, although he had taken our name. Yes, 'twas a good work, I tell thee. Take away thine accusing eyes—thy blue, English, heretic eyes—Ned Trueman; why dost thou come

IRON-STANCHIONED: *iron-barred*

to torment me because I tried to save thee from purgatory and perdition?" And the poor old woman became so excited that Conrad and his mother could with difficulty soothe her.

Old Ned Trueman, who stood by the half-opened door, listening to every word she uttered, could scarcely be restrained from going in and reproaching her.

"Nay, nay! do not be so harsh to my poor old grandam; she hath—"

"Harsh!" repeated the old man, "she hath murdered my son! Harsh, forsooth! Hast thou any thought for thy murdered father?"

"Thou knowest that I have! Ah! thou knowest not how I have longed to see him; but I know, too, that my grandam hath done this evil deed, believing that it was good, since her confessor told her it was needful for the Church and for the salvation of his soul."

But Ned Trueman shook his head. "'Twas base and cruel, and how could she believe it was good?"

"Thou art a Lollard now, and canst doubt many things that the Church accounteth good; but it was not always so with thee. Thou didst hate the Lollards aforetime; and wherefore was it but because the Church called them evil and seditious, and thou deemedst that the Church must be right? Even so my grandam believed, and when her confessor told her she could save my father's soul, and

PERDITION: *hell*
BASE: *cowardly*

turn away the disgrace from the old name of von Zitka by delivering him over to be reconciled to the Church, she believed it was a good and noble work she was called to do. The Church hath blinded men's eyes and perverted their consciences. She hath "put darkness for light," and "called evil good;"[1] and my grandam hath but believed her, and followed her teaching, as a silly sheep, witless and helpless."

But it was some time before the old man could look upon the matter in this light. His son had been murdered by these persecuting black friars, whose chief mission in the world was the extirpation of heresy. In his anger against Dame Ursula, he forgot his own part in the affair—that his hardness and harshness had driven his son away.

But it soon became evident that Dame Ursula would not long be a source of altercation, for after the unusual excitement following upon the recital of what had so long been a mystery both to Conrad and his mother, her strength began visibly to decline. Once or twice when Dame Ermengarde was bending over her the pale thin lips moved, and she murmured, "Forgive, Ermengarde! Forgive, Edward! It was a good work, a very good work. Lord Jesus, forgive!" and murmuring these last words, she died, a week after she had divulged the secret that so long lay hidden in her own heart.

As soon as Dame Ursula was buried, Conrad and his mother, with Ned Trueman, began to

[1] Isaiah 5:20
EXTIRPATION: *destruction*
ALTERCATION: *conflict*

prepare for their journey to Bohemia. As it was uncertain how long they might be gone, or whether they would ever return to England again, this necessarily took up some time; for Conrad had to go to Lutterworth for the final settlement of some business there, and to obtain some more of Dr. Wycliffe's books to take with him to his native land. Ned Trueman also had some affairs to settle; for the money he had saved, in the hope of one day being able to purchase some land, he now resolved to take with him to rescue his son, if he was still living; and so there were several visits to the Lombard merchants, who were the chief bankers of London.

Then last, but not least, there were the visits to friends—to Master Winchester and his gentle niece, Mary, who promised to write to Conrad, and tell him all that befell her uncle and her dear cousin, Dame Margery Gilpin. Master Filpot, the armorer, in spite of worldly prosperity and the increase of his business, talked about selling all his armor at reduced prices, and giving up his smithy, to go with them; and Dame Ermengarde urged him to do so.

"England is no longer a safe abiding-place, since this new law hath been passed for the burning of heretics," she said; "and I would that my Conrad were beyond the sea, for he is overbold in speech, and avoweth to all men that he is a Lollard."

"Nay, nay, my daughter; this new law is but a

trick of Archbishop Arundel to frighten men out of Lollardism; and doubtless many will be more punctual in paying all the Church dues and going to confession, so that others may rest in peace."

Others may have rested in the same hope, but it was soon dispelled. Before their preparations were completed they heard the startling news that the preacher of St. Osyth, Master William Sawtree, whom Conrad had met at Dame Gilpin's, had been arrested for refusing to worship the cross or the bread in the sacrament. Another charge was that he had declared a priest was more bound to preach the Word of God than to recite particular services at certain canonical hours.

That his condemnation was decided upon almost before he was arrested soon became apparent; and all that his friends could do for him at his trial was useless. He was condemned by Archbishop Arundel; and, with the hypocrisy that marked all the doings of the Church, he was handed over to the secular power, with the recommendation that he should be dealt with mercifully.

Mercifully! when every nerve had been strained by the Church to secure the passing of the infamous Act of Parliament by which it became lawful to burn heretics; and then, so soon as it became a law, this defenseless victim was seized, that the Lollards might know it was to be no vain threat, but a terrible engine for the suppression of all freedom of speech and conscience, and even thought.

CANONICAL HOURS: *times appointed by the church*

The news of the condemnation of Master William Sawtree hastened the departure of our friends. The day that the first martyr-fire was lighted in Smithfield they sailed from the port of London, Dame Ermengarde covering her eyes, lest she should see the sparks and the glare of the flames, as they slowly floated down with the tide toward London Bridge, where the vessel lay that was to carry them from Church-oppressed England.

Chapter XVI

In Prague

THE journey from England to Bohemia four hundred years ago was an undertaking fraught with considerable danger and difficulty; and so it was with a feeling of deep thankfulness that they looked upon the walls and battlements of Bohemia's capital, the city of Prague.

Conrad, of course, had no recollection of his birthplace; but his mother could not restrain her tears when they came within sight of the gates which she had last passed through in the train of Queen Anne; while her father-in-law, the English mason, thought of nothing but where the Dominican monastery could be in which he hoped to find his son.

Conrad was quite as anxious as his grandfather to ascertain what his father's fate had been; but he could sympathize somewhat in his mother's feelings on this her first return to her native city. He wondered where and how she would find the friends she had talked of as being likely to aid her in their search for her husband; for, although she had heard of these occasionally during the lifetime of her mistress, since the queen's death news had come to her but rarely.

They put up at a hostelry near the gate, and while his mother and grandfather went to rest after the fatigue of their last day's journey, Conrad went out to see something of his native city, and listen to scraps of talk falling from one and another as they passed.

It was a curious habit that he had formed at Lutterworth; but by it he had been able to gauge pretty accurately the drift of public opinion on any topic of public interest. They had heard during their journey of the deposition of the King of Bohemia from being Emperor of Germany. He had succeeded his father, Charles IV, in the imperial dignity; but the slumbering jealousy of the Teuton States against the insulated Sclavonic stranger—Bohemia—which, though numbered with them as a federation, was not of them either in language, thought, or feeling—found expression in the votes of the Rhine electors, who took the imperial crown from King Wenzel, to give it to one of their own nationality.

Of course, Bohemia felt herself insulted in the person of her king, who still retained his hereditary kingdom; and, knowing this, Conrad soon began to understand how it was that in all the parties of students he met, a Bohemian was rarely

IMPERIAL DIGNITY: *position of Emperor*
INSULATED: *isolated*
SCLAVONIC: *an Eastern European people group*

to be seen conversing with a German. The University of Prague was one of the most renowned in Europe, and drew thousands of young men to its halls of learning, especially from the neighboring German States. Germans, Poles, and Bohemians formed the majority of the students, though there were a few French and English; and hitherto they had lived together harmoniously enough.

But the deposition of King Wenzel seemed to have roused in the breasts of both German and Bohemian students the same conflicting passions that agitated their nations. The Germans were now singing songs of triumph at the deposition of the Bohemian king from the imperial throne, while the insulted Bohemians vented their wrath and indignation against their stolid neighbors on every occasion that presented itself.

As Conrad wandered through the streets, gazing at the splendid palaces, and loitered on the bridge, watching the water flowing through its arches as he rested against the parapet, he heard more than one party of students mention a name that seemed to be the center of conflicting opinions in Prague just now. John Huss, one of the university preachers, seemed to be as popular among the Bohemian students as King Wenzel himself, and equally unpopular among their German companions. Conrad felt curious to know something of this strange popularity and dislike;

STOLID: *unemotional*
PARAPET: *low railing*

but he resolved to wait until he had found his old friend, Master Jerome Faulfisch, who could, doubtless, tell him all about it.

Meanwhile he and his grandfather went in search of the Dominican monastery, where his father had first been taken; while Dame Ermengarde set about finding a suitable abode, for to live at the hostelry beyond a few days was quite out of the question. Like everyone else who has left a city for some years, she found so many changes had taken place during her absence, that she felt almost a stranger where she had previously been familiar with every house in the neighborhood and had had many friends among the citizens. In nothing was this more marked than in the question of house-rent, which had increased to almost double. Dame Ermengarde soon became convinced that she must relinquish the idea of living near her former home, in the neighborhood of the palace, and, of course, the most aristocratic portion of Prague, and retreat to one of the outlying districts, near one of the gates, where rents were sure to be cheaper.

Trueman had wished to live somewhere near the Dominican monastery, for he had taken up the idea that his son was still alive and concealed within its walls; but Conrad, wishing to please his mother in their choice of a home, had favored the idea of living in the neighborhood of the palace—more especially since he had heard that John Huss was confessor to Queen Sophia, and court preacher, too.

But, of course, as their united means, added to what he might earn as a teacher, would still be but limited, he saw the wisdom of following his grandfather's plan now; and so a house was taken, commanding a view of the gate of the Dominican monastery. Grim and gaunt rose the massive pile of buildings, with their grated loophole windows and iron-stanchioned doors; and hardly less grim-looking were the black-robed friars, as they crept in and out of the narrow doorway, all day long coming and going with silent, death-like tread, and yet with ceaseless energy. These followers of Dominic de Guzman were all-powerful here, as everywhere else, and still followed pre-eminently the work laid down for them by their founder—the extirpation of heresy. No craft, no guile, no wickedness, was too great for them, if heresy was to be detected or checked; and if one of these clever friars had been told that a simple old Englishman had set himself the task of outwitting them in some of their plans, they would certainly have deemed him a lunatic.

But that was just what old Trueman had set himself to do; and he began his work the very day they arrived at their new home. In portioning out the house, the old man chose a room for himself where he could sit at the window and watch the coming and going of every monk and every stranger whose business brought them to the

CRAFT: *deception*
GUILE: *cunning, treachery*

Master Trueman's Room

monastery. To sit and watch ceaselessly day after day, until he grew to recognize some of the brethren, as he caught glimpses of their faces—this, for the present, seemed to be the old man's plan.

Conrad went to work in a different way. He walked about in the neighborhood of the university, watching every group of students who passed him, in the hope of recognizing Jerome Faulfisch among them. But, although he heard his name mentioned once in connection with that of Huss, he did not encounter his old friend.

His timidity prevented him from asking any of the students about Faulfisch for some time; but at length he resolved to do so, for his mother had failed to trace him among her friends; and so, stationing himself near the university, he at last addressed a party of Bohemians who were rushing toward the Bethlehem Chapel.

"Faulfisch—Jerome Faulfisch—why, he is a friend of Master John Huss, and will, doubtless, be at the Bethlehem Chapel today, to hear him preach. Wilt thou come and hear him, too?"

"Ah, that will I right gladly," answered Conrad, for he felt curious to hear the man about whom there were such conflicting reports, as well as anxious to see his friend. It was not easy to obtain a seat when it was known that Huss was going to preach; but by the courtesy of his student friends he was accommodated, although they had to stand themselves.

Conrad recalled the time when he first looked upon the bold, lion-like countenance of Dr. Wycliffe, with its keen, penetrating gaze, and somehow he felt disappointed with the personal appearance of Huss. To judge by this, he was a man neither very bold nor very penetrating in intellect, but highly conscientious; more cautious than quick in adopting new views of truth, and yet, withal, firm in his attachments when once made.

It was not to be expected that Conrad should think the preaching of Huss equal to his great Master Wycliffe; but he could not wonder at the city going half-mad about her wonderful preacher; for, truly, the discourse of Huss was wonderful in those days—wonderful for its eloquence and

GAINSAY: *deny*

clearness, and also for the boldness with which he denounced the sins of clergy and people alike. He spared neither bishops nor courtiers, but lashed their sins with an unsparing hand.

"He practiceth what he doth preach, too," whispered one of Conrad's friends into his ear.

"He is a man of virtuous life, I trow," said Conrad.

"No one can gainsay it," replied another. "At first he preached against citizens and courtiers only—against cheating and taking of usury, and luxury and pride; but he soon learned to see that in these things the wickedness of the clergy exceeded that of courtiers and citizens; and so now he doth tell all men that, except they repent, they shall all likewise perish. This is new and unsavory doctrine for the clergy, I trow," added the student.

But before Conrad could answer someone else touched him upon the shoulder, and, turning quickly, he was face to face with Jerome Faulfisch.

The congregation were dispersing, and the party of students had lingered on account of Conrad's lameness, for there was sure to be a crush at the doors; and, thus lingering, Faulfisch had time to confirm an idea that he had had the moment he saw Conrad—that he had seen the pale, delicate-looking stranger before.

"Master Faulfisch, I have been looking for thee ever since I came to Prague!" exclaimed Conrad, in a tone of delight.

"I have been away from Prague for some weeks.

USURY: *interest on loans*
UNSAVORY: *unpleasant*

But call me not Faulfisch, but Jerome," he added; and then, thanking the students for their care of him, he led him by a different door out into a quiet back street.

"Now tell me all about my English friends," said Master Jerome; "how fareth it with Sir John Oldcastle?"

"He is still pursuing the study of arms, and hopes to do good service for King Henry, as well as to be the faithful servant of our Master in heaven."

"I am greatly rejoiced to hear thee say this. And now what hath brought thee to Bohemia at this time? As I wrote thee in my letters, I have sought to learn tidings of thy father, but cannot hear more than this: he was taken to the Dominican monastery, and hath not since been heard of."

"And the Dominicans—what do they say about it? for I have come to Prague on purpose to find my father, and will do so if it be possible," said Conrad.

Jerome shook his head. "If thou hast ever had aught to do with these black friars, thou knowest they are more crafty than any of their brethren, if such a thing be possible. I have seen the prior and many of the brethren upon this business, but all declare they know naught of such a person ever having come to their holy house; and I doubt not they will tell thee the same, giving thee fair promises to make search concerning the business."

"But I shall make my inquiries outside first, before applying to the prior. Did I tell thee I had found my father's father, and that he had come to Prague with us to find his son?"

"I had not heard it; but 'tis well thou hast told me, for he and thou must alike be cautious, if his name be Trueman."

"And wherefore is there so great need of caution?" asked Conrad.

"Because many in Prague remember thy father's name to this day—remember him as one of the most daring followers of Conrad Strickna—after whom thou art named, I doubt not—and Matthias Janovius. These two were preachers as popular in their day as Master Huss now is, and they complained as loudly as he does of the spiritual death and desolation everywhere prevailing through the corruptions of the Church. I was only a boy then, but I can remember seeing thy father a short time before our hasty flight from Prague, and of the exhortation he gave us to hold fast by the truth, though we yielded our lives in its defense. The persecution of Janovius and his followers had already commenced, for the clergy were specially indignant at his teaching that the sacrament ought to be administered in both kinds; and when, at length, he made use of the favor in which he was held by the Emperor Charles, our king, to urge him to call a general council for the reformation of the Church, their fury knew no bounds. The emperor was prevailed upon to banish Janovius; and many, like my father, left Bohemia with him. Others, hoping they and their opinions might be forgotten or overlooked, remained behind; and upon them the full fury of the storm burst. They were robbed, beaten, drowned in the river, and at last burned as evil heretics. Thy father, doubtless, thought to escape through the favor in which thy mother was held by the Princess Anne, who herself favored these doctrines, as thou hast doubtless heard; and it was through this, I trow, that he was so secretly carried away."

"Then my namesake, Conrad Strickna, was somewhat like Dr. Wycliffe in his teaching?"

"It may be that he had seen some of Wycliffe's writings, and learned to discern the truth from them, even as Master Huss hath done since. Thou dost remember thy work of copying and translating, Conrad?"

"Ah, they were happy days at Lutterworth!" exclaimed Conrad, with something of a sigh; "I would that I had profited more by them."

"Thou wilt be glad to hear that thy work in those days was not in vain. I brought all the writings thou didst help me to pack safely here to Prague; and meeting with Master Huss, who was even then earnestly seeking for more enlightenment than the Church could give, I besought him to read them, and now—shall I tell thee?—Huss will carry on the work Wycliffe hath begun!"

Chapter XVII

John Huss

THE friendship of Jerome and Conrad increased daily; and the latter was found to be a most valuable coadjutor in the work of disseminating the purer truths of the Gospel which he and Huss had set themselves to accomplish—the one by preaching and teaching, both at court and in the university, and the other by spreading the bold and convincing writings of Dr. Wycliffe among all classes in Bohemia. Conrad's old work of translating the English writings of Wycliffe into Bohemian was again taken up, while copies of his Latin treatises were being multiplied by many of the students in the university.

But although Conrad's time and energy were thus fully occupied, he by no means neglected the errand which had brought him and his grandfather to Bohemia. By the advice of Jerome, the old man had consented to abandon his name for the present, and he was known among their friends as Mason, or the mason—no one seemed sure about

COADJUTOR: *assistant*
DISSEMINATING: *spreading*
TREATISES: *writings*

which he should of right be called; but few of them knew the secret of his real name, or why he had left England. The old man was very silent upon the subject of his hopes and fears—the recovery of his long-lost son; and no one but Conrad and his mother understood why it was that he sat, day after day, alone at the window, silently watching the monastery gate opposite.

After a few months of this silent watching he took the bolder step of standing at the door, and often giving alms to one and another of the black-robed brotherhood; but it might also be noticed that he peered closely and curiously under every cowl, while he transferred the coin from his own pouch to the outstretched hand.

After this had gone on for some time he prevailed upon Dame Ermengarde to provide more food every day than they could possibly consume themselves; and with this for an excuse, he often got one of the friars to come in and chat with him, for he had learned something of the Bohemian tongue by this time.

All this, going on close to the monastery gate, could not escape the notice of the superior; and, as he so frequently gave alms, a notion soon got afloat among the brethren that the strange old Englishman was immensely rich, and must be pleased and patronized accordingly; for that his wealth must be left to their monastery was a foregone conclusion.

To gain admission to the chapel, or even some of the private services of the friars, was a matter of small difficulty after this; and Dame Ermengarde herself was almost deceived by the old man's seeming fondness for the black friars.

"Conrad, thou knowest I am as anxious as thou art to find thy father, and I have made many inquiries, even sending a message to King Wenzel himself, beseeching him for the love he bore his sister, my mistress, to make search for my husband, and—"

"Nay, my mother; but the king cannot help us, I trow," interrupted Conrad.

"He can do more than thy grandfather, for he is bewitched by these black friars," replied Dame Ermengarde, angrily. Then, in a more anxious tone, she said, "I have heard that monks and friars do sometimes, in their grasping after unknown things, learn how to commune with Satan, who soon becomes their master, by imparting to them secrets by which they can gain the mastery over other men, even robbing them of their senses, or making them believe and love what they aforetime hated. This, I fear, is now being worked upon thy poor grandfather."

Conrad looked alarmed, for Dame Ermengarde had only expressed the general belief of that age, and even the best and most enlightened men were not free from this dread of witchcraft.

"Can it be that these friars have discovered our secret, and learned who we are by means of this black art—this alchemy, as some call it?" exclaimed Conrad; and he resolved to watch his grandfather, and, if possible, draw him from his all-absorbing interest in these black friars. Nothing was to be gained in the way of clearing up the mystery that surrounded his father's fate by that means, he felt sure; and he blamed himself now for not trying to convince his grandfather of the futility of this plan before. The fact was that as Conrad's hopes diminished after each vain effort he had made, he felt thankful that the old man had taken up a plan of action that involved a long, slow, patient watch; for, while he was watching he was hoping, and he would not have the old man robbed of his dearly-cherished hopes, or know the pain and suffering he often endured at the failure of plan after plan. Such pain and such failure would bring sickness and death to his grandfather, he felt sure; for he had no other object in life; nothing to think of in the way of occupation, but this patient, dogged, persistent watching of the monastery and its inmates.

It was, therefore, no easy matter for Conrad even to try and persuade his grandfather to give up this occupation, and with it his dearly-cherished plans; but he thought it to be his duty now; and, therefore, he would not shrink from it much longer.

An opportunity soon offered, for the old man came indoors one day with the news that there had been a fight on the bridge between some German and Bohemian students.

"Who told thee?" asked Conrad, looking up from his work of writing.

"The friars barely escaped receiving some of the blows as they passed," answered the old man.

"I would not believe any tale that a friar chose to tell. I wish I could go and find out the truth of this for myself; but I have promised Master Huss he shall have this treatise tonight; but thou couldst go," he added, looking at his grandfather.

He shook his head. "I cannot leave my post for twenty fights," he said, preparing to leave the room as he spoke. But Conrad laid his hand on his arm, and detained him.

"I—I am afraid thou art under some evil spell, Grandfather," said Conrad, tenderly.

The old man laughed half-derisively, half-angrily. "Thou dost fear *I* am bewitched? Nay, nay; I am bewitching them, Conrad. They think me a foolish, crazy old man, gone mad about mason's work and the cunning contriving of buildings. Perhaps they think they are bewitching me; but I am learning, Conrad—learning all about the mason-work in the monastery. They show me a bit now and a bit then, first one and then the other, sometimes a cell or a corridor, then a pointed arch and a staircase cut of solid stone; and I talk of the stone until they think me one, too; but I am learning, Conrad—I am learning."

"But what art thou learning?" asked his grandson, as a new fear darted across his mind; for, if not bewitched, the constant thinking of this one subject had certainly turned his brain, and he was in very truth going mad, as he wished the friars to believe.

"Learning?" repeated the old man. "What is it I want to learn, but to find my way in and out of the monastery, through all its winding passages and stairways, until I can go without fear, and find my boy—my long-lost son?"

Conrad looked his surprise at the wild scheme his grandfather had proposed, and was more than ever concerned about his mental condition; but he saw that it would be useless to say anything about this now. He resolved, however, to keep his grandfather and his movements more in his mind than he had done of late; and then, finding he could not settle to his work again, he went out to ascertain the cause of the students' fight on the bridge.

On his way he met his friend Jerome, and asked him what it all meant—whether the disturbance was serious, or merely a slight brawl.

Jerome shook his head sadly. "It is the first fight outside the university walls; but I greatly fear it will not be the last. Hast thou not heard the news that all Prague is ringing with just now?"

Conrad shook his head. "I have not been out for more than a week," he said.

"And no one hath told thee of the archbishop's threat—that any who dare to teach the doctrines of Wycliffe shall die the death of heretics, at the stake? Master Huss knoweth well enough that it is against him this threat is issued, for, although he began by thinking Wycliffe a heretic, he hath learned from his writings to love the truth he taught, and hath begun to teach the same here in Prague, which hath, of course, alarmed the archbishop; and now, to widen the breach, the German professors of the university are openly taking sides with the archbishop as orthodox against heretics; while the Bohemians, remembering that it was the German episcopal votes that deprived King Wenzel of his imperial crown, have taken the side of Master Huss and freedom of conscience; and, from the sullen jealousy that has so long existed between the two, this act of the archbishop hath evolved open strife; and what may follow none can tell."

It was plain that Master Jerome thought the matter a serious one; but Conrad did not understand it sufficiently to share his anxieties. "Surely the council now sitting at Pisa will amend all this," he said, hopefully.

"I know not what to think. As thou knowest, the council hath deposed both the rival popes; and Master Huss preached yesterday against their arrogance, calling them evil men, who stirred up strife and schism; but the archbishop still adheres

ORTHODOX: *holding traditional beliefs*
EPISCOPAL: *bishops'*

to Gregory, and hath appealed to the king today to stop our bold preacher; but the king only shook his head, and smiled as he answered, 'So long as Master Huss preached against us of the world, you rejoiced, and declared that the Spirit of God spoke in him.' Now it is your turn."

Conrad clapped his hands in triumph.

"Master Huss has nothing to fear, then, from the archbishop's threats, since the king taketh sides with him; wherefore, then, art thou so anxious, Master Jerome?"

"Dost thou not see, Conrad, that Huss is making foes with a power greater than that possessed by any king? Just now the long-talked-of council is sitting at Pisa; and the king, with Huss, hath taken sides with the council against the deposed popes; but what it may be when another pope is chosen none can tell."

"But will not the council amend the corruptions of the Church, and bid her teach the Gospel, instead of the fables and lying inventions preached by the monks?"

"Many hope it will be so; but I know not what to think," answered Jerome; and then, after some further conversation, the friends parted; and Conrad returned home to tell his mother what he had heard concerning these public affairs, and what he feared for his grandfather.

The next day there was another fight with the students; and these grew so frequent during the next few months that the university was in a state of feud, and was the constant scene of polemical strife scarcely less disgraceful than the faction fights in the street. It was German against Bohemian, Churchman against Wycliffite—a political and religious warfare—until at last the Germans, to the number of thirty thousand, with their professors, abandoned the university and the city, betaking themselves to Leipsic.

The citizens felt the loss of their German customers severely; but Huss did not lose his popularity. He became rector of the university, and preached more boldly than ever the doctrines of Wycliffe; and Conrad grew confident that the sad forebodings of Jerome were without the least foundation.

"England hath cast from her this offer of the Gospel; but Bohemia is receiving it gladly," he said, one day when Jerome called.

"The people of Bohemia would gladly have received the teaching of Strickna and Janovius, as they now do that of Huss; but the Church silenced them, and persecuted their followers, as they will us by-and-by, if they have but the power. Hast thou had news from England of late?"

"I had a letter from Dame Margery Gilpin, bearing sad tidings of the persecution against the Lollards. Master Sawtree's martyrdom was the first for this truth of God—this good news He hath sent to the world—that the Lord Jesus hath borne our sins and carried our sorrows; that *He* is our Savior, and not our good works, or penances, or wealth."

"And the people of England—did they not receive these glad tidings, that would set them free from the cruel slavery of the Church?" asked Jerome.

"Yea, truly; and many of them are now suffering imprisonment and the loss of all things, while all live in fear and dread of what may come upon them, reading God's Word only in secret, and hiding it as though it were an evil thing; while others are called upon to prove their love of this truth by dying a most cruel and shameful death. Ah! say not the *people* of England refused the Gospel; but her king, in fear of the Church, hath rejected it; and the Church is binding her galling yoke more fast upon him and his people."

Conrad spoke passionately, for the remembrance of Dame Margery's letter, with its account of how many of their friends had suffered and were suffering, was fresh in his mind.

"And thou canst tell me this of England, and what the Church is doing there, and yet hope for Bohemia?" exclaimed Jerome.

"King Wenzel hath taken sides with Master Huss, and the great council hath been called at last that is to reform the Church; and it may be that the council will decree that the teaching of Dr. Wycliffe was not heresy, but the very truth of God, and command that the Church shall teach the same, and that all bishops and priests shall live

GALLING: *irritating*

pure and blameless lives, like our godly Master Huss and Dr. Wycliffe."

But Jerome shook his head. "Many have hoped for this, but I cannot. How can a clean thing come out of an unclean? The Church is wholly corrupt, I fear, and will not be amended by the council except as it may receive the pope it shall choose. This done, it will break up, and the cries of God's people will still go up to His throne, 'Lord, how long wilt Thou suffer this? O Lord, how long?'"

But Conrad hoped more from the Council of Pisa than this, and was ready to laugh at his friend for his fears, believing that in Bohemia, at least, the Gospel would be triumphant, and from her it would spread to all lands, until, sanctioned and taught by those who now so bitterly opposed it, the reformation would at last come for which the world had so long watched and waited in vain.

Chapter XVIII

The Monastery of the Black Friars

A SILENCE almost as of death brooded over the capital of Bohemia, the famous city of Prague; and a traveler approaching it by way of the White Mountain, just outside the city gates, wondered what dreadful calamity could have befallen, for not a *matin* bell had been heard to ring that morning, and the few citizens who passed in and out seemed to creep along, as if weighed down with a calamity too heavy to be borne.

The traveler himself was not too elate, for it was our old friend Conrad, returning from a visit to England; and he brought with him the sad news that the persecution against the Lollards raged more fiercely than ever; so that the silence and gloom that seemed to have settled down upon his native city increased his depression still more. He hastened home through the silent, almost deserted streets, and it was a relief to him when his mother opened the door and clasped him in her arms. The next minute his grandfather came

MATIN: *morning prayer*
ELATE: *joyful*

forward, looking well and cheerful, so that there was no need to ask how he fared; indeed, the old man followed Conrad when he went up to his own room, assuring him that he never felt better in his life. Conrad felt puzzled at his grandfather's manner, and again there came a doubt of his sanity; but this was quickly dispelled when, the door being closed, he came close to him and whispered, "Canst thou bear to hear good news, Conrad?"

"Good news! my mother saith there is naught but evil tidings in Prague."

"Dame Ermengarde doth not know all that is being done in Prague; she is but a woman, and therefore not to be trusted."

Conrad felt rather angry at this implied slight of his mother; but his grandfather seemed so impatient to tell his news that Conrad would not stop to argue the point just now; but he did not pay much heed to the old man's talk of the wonderful mason's work he had been doing at the monastery, until he said, "And I have seen *him,* Conrad!"

"Seen who? Master Huss, my master?"

"Nay, nay, I have seen my son—my son, Ned—thy father!"

Conrad forgot his lameness, and actually sprang from his seat and tottered to his grandfather's side without crutches.

"Tell me that again! Oh, tell me it is true, and that my father is alive!" he gasped, holding by the old man's arm.

"Hush, hush! I would not have thy mother hear this; no, not if it would take the interdict from the city," said the mason; and he led Conrad back to his seat, and implored him to be calm. "Thou art worse than I was when I saw him, though I had to lean against the wall, or I should have fallen."

"Where didst thou see him?" asked Conrad.

"Where could I but in the monastery, where he is kept a close prisoner? I have undertaken to oversee some mason-work; and, to my great joy, one of those set to carry the rubbish away was my boy."

"And he knew thee, or didst thou tell him thou wert his father?"

"Nay, I told him I was a friend; for what had I ever done to deserve the name of father?" and the old man sighed. "I told him I had known him when he was in the world, and would fain help him now; but at first he shook his head, thinking I was his enemy. At last my heart would speak, and when we were alone I snatched the shovel out of his hand, that he was clearing the rubbish away with, and throwing my arms round his neck, I said, 'Oh, Ned, my boy, my boy, I have found you at last!' but he was so weak from being shut up there so long that he fainted in my arms. Oh, Conrad, they have well-nigh killed him, and I doubt whether any but his father would have known him again; and I know not now whether he remembers me, or that he is not, as ye deemed me, mad—mad from the long silence in which he hath lived!" and the poor old man paced up and down the room in such strong excitement that Conrad began to fear whether the whole story was not a wild fancy after all, and that his grandfather's brain had succumbed to the long strain of constantly dwelling on one idea. He resolved, therefore, not to hope too much from what he had just heard, but to talk to his grandfather on other subjects before returning to this again. His mother, calling at this moment, enabled him to carry out this resolution; and he willingly promised not to divulge his grandfather's secret to anyone at present.

"Thy grandfather hath told thee all the news, I trow," said Dame Ermengarde, rather discontentedly.

For a moment Conrad looked confused, until he suddenly remembered that his grandfather had told him the startling news that the city was under an interdict, and he exclaimed, "I cannot understand what I have heard; surely the city is not under the ban of the Church!"

But Dame Ermengarde tremblingly confirmed the news. "There have been no funerals, no baptisms, no marriages, no *matin* or *vesper* services for more than a week. It is awful to dwell in a city of silence, without even a convent bell to ring the sacred hours, or a church door to be opened. Even the street noises seem sad and subdued now, and no one leaves the house unless necessarily."

"But wherefore is all this?" asked Conrad.

"Hast thou not heard? Master Jerome sent thee a letter by a merchant journeying to London, in which—"

"The letter was brought with all speed and safety, and told of the vendors of indulgences coming to Prague with a special bull from the pope authorizing the sale of these licenses for sin, and how Jerome had publicly burned the same under the gallows."

"Ah! 'twas a right brave thing to do; and the people did their work well afterward, for they drove the sin-mongers out of Prague at last!" interrupted his grandfather.

"But I was sore afraid, Conrad—more afraid than when the archbishop's messenger came here and carried off all the works of Dr. Wycliffe thou hadst copied, for the rioters stormed the courthouse at last, when the magistrate would fain protect the indulgence merchants."

"And how fareth it with the three ambassadors who have journeyed to Rome to answer the citation sent to Master Huss? Have they returned?"

"Nay; it is for this very thing the city now lieth under an interdict, I trow," replied Dame Ermengarde, with a sigh.

"It is for Master Huss, and his teaching the doctrines of Dr. Wycliffe," repeated Conrad.

"Ah! I would that I had never heard the word 'heresy' or the name of Wycliffe!" exclaimed Dame Ermengarde. "Our great preacher, Master Huss, hath been publicly excommunicated, and obliged to leave the city. Thou didst think that when there was a council of the Church the reformation would begin; but 'tis said that the present pope hath lived, and doth live, a more evil life than any that went before him, and careth nothing for the Church, except how he may enrich himself and persecute all accused of heresy;" and the lady sighed deeply.

Conrad could say little to comfort his mother. Surely the future looked dark indeed for those who, no longer satisfied with the superstitions and corruptions of the Church of Rome, had sought, in the purer doctrines taught by Wycliffe and Huss, the light and knowledge of God. He had been revealed as the Lord, gracious and merciful, who would not give His glory to another, even the most exalted saint, but had given His Son to be the one Mediator between God and man—the one perfect sacrifice—by which He sought to reconcile the world to Himself. Believing these truths of the Gospel, how could they join in saint and image-worship, or trust in the mass as a sacrifice for sin, to be repeated each time the words of consecration were uttered by the priest over the bread and wine?

Huss had begun to follow the teaching of his predecessor, Matthias Janovius, by giving to all his communicants the cup in the sacrament, which struck at the root of transubstantiation, and the teachings of those who, with the authority of the

COMMUNICANTS: *church members*

Church, declared that after the words of blessing the bread is turned into the very body, bones, blood, and divinity of the Lord Jesus Christ; and about this, of course, there were the low mutterings of a coming storm.

It soon came out, too, that Dame Ermengarde had another cause of sorrow—had had another disappointment. A distant relative of her family had lately been appointed as chamberlain to King Wenzel, and she, having ascertained that he, like most of the court, was a follower of Huss, paid him a visit, and besought him to intercede with the king, that some further inquiries might be made concerning her husband's fate. Zisca had promised to do this, but nothing had come of it yet; for the king already had enough on his hands, and was half-afraid of protecting Huss, for fear of giving mortal offense to the court of Rome. He was glad that Huss had withdrawn from the city, and was too anxious for the interdict to be removed to inquire too closely into the mystery of a man's disappearance thirty years before. So Dame Ermengarde's newly-raised hopes were again disappointed; and at present Conrad could not tell her of his grandfather's secret, for he could hardly believe in its truth himself.

It was well, perhaps, that he could not realize this all at once, or his impatience to see his father might have tempted him to some rash deed that would have frustrated all his grandfather was trying to accomplish. The old man had assumed the entire supervision of the work going on inside the monastery; and to secure the services of one who was a thorough master of his work, and yet not only gave his services free of cost, but was humored and pleased that they were accepted, was a stroke of policy that the superior prided himself upon accomplishing; so he had free access to the interior, could employ whom he pleased to assist those who came with him to do the skilled labor, and enjoyed an amount of freedom in his intercourse with the brethren rarely accorded to any stranger.

That he should keep the silent, patient, hard-working lay brother Sebastian near him excited no comment from the rest of the brethren; for, in spite of his reticence, he was a favorite with everybody except the superior and a few of the older monks, who always shunned him, set him the hardest and most menial tasks, but otherwise never interfered with him.

Brother Sebastian never went outside the monastery gates, the brethren said, when they were asked about this; and at the mention of this fact he looked up, and seemed to show some interest in what was being said, so that his father resolved to try this avenue of communication with him, since all others seemed closed, and he had no recollection of their first interview.

"Thou wouldst like to see the world outside the gates," he said, when they were left to themselves.

INTERCOURSE: *interaction*
RETICENCE: *quietness, reserved manner*

The poor drudge nodded. "I would I could see Master Janovius," he replied, in a low, sepulchral voice, and looking round cautiously as he spoke.

His father almost trembled with hope and anxiety as he said, "Thou dost know Master Janovius, I trow."

Again came the assenting nod, and something like brightness shone for a moment in the dulled eyes. "I forget everything he taught us—everything but this, Jesus died for sinners."

"Thou wilt not be able to see Master Janovius; but I will bring thee words he hath writ, an thou would like to see them."

Again came the gleam of intelligence into the dulled eyes, as he murmured, "I forget—forget everything."

As soon as the old man went home he begged Conrad to obtain something written by Janovius, if it were possible; and this request did at last convince him that his grandfather was not resting his hopes merely on a wild notion, as he supposed. He soon obtained what the old man asked for; it was a simple letter, written in defense of giving the wine in the sacrament to all communicants; and Conrad speedily made a copy of it on a slip of parchment, that could be rolled up and easily concealed.

To describe Brother Sebastian's joy when he received this would be impossible. He kissed it as soon as he had read the first lines, and then he threw his arms around his father's neck and kissed

SEPULCHRAL: *hollow, tomblike*

him. "I know—I know! I remember all now," he said.

"Dost thou know me, Ned? know thy old father from London city?"

But at this question Brother Sebastian started back. "My father!" he repeated; "nay, nay, talk not of him; I have angered him, and he will never forgive me."

"He was a harsh, stern man, then, Ned; he knew naught of mercy and little of love in those days."

The old man spoke in English now, and at the sound of the old familiar words the monk-drudge started as though he had been stung. "Who—who art thou?" he said, speaking in the same language, his dull eyes gleaming with unwonted light; "who art thou, to speak to me of my father and call him harsh? I tell thee I left him. I was willful and disobedient. How sayest thou my father was harsh?"

It pleased the old man to hear his son speak in this way; and yet it seemed that now he had hopelessly offended him, for during the rest of that day he studiously obeyed every command that was given him, but carefully avoided any further communication.

The next day, however, he gave signs of a further return of memory; for as soon as he and his father were left alone he said, "I have read the wonderful words of Master Janovius, and thou mayest tell him I remember now—remember all he told us last week. Dost thou know the Princess Anne? she is soon to be Queen of England, they say; and then I shall go back with Dame Ermengarde, my wife, in the train of the princess; and, now that I have a little son to show my father, surely he will forgive me for going beyond seas to seek my fortune."

"Yes, yes, he will forgive thee, Ned!" said the old man, brushing away the tears as he spoke. How he restrained the wrath he felt against those who had reduced his son to this almost imbecile state he did not know; how he could speak smooth, fair words to the superior, and give alms of money and food to the gossiping brethren who daily oppressed his son, was a puzzle the old man could never solve. Only the yearning love he felt for his son, who needed his watchfulness and care now more, even, than when he was a child, enabled him to pass through this trying ordeal without betraying his secret; for it was still a secret shared only with Conrad, for as yet it was deemed unsafe to trust even Dame Ermengarde with the news that her husband still lived.

The times were perilous, and enemies were ever on the alert. Huss was still absent from Prague; and though a traveler named Jacobel brought tidings that he was preaching in every town and village throughout Bohemia the wonderful Gospel of Jesus Christ, in place of the wild legends of the monks, still he was regarded as a heretic, and the ban of excommunication yet rested upon him.

IMBECILE: *feeble-minded*

Chapter XIX

The Last First

CONRAD was most anxious to see his father, and waited with eager impatience the return of his grandfather each day from the monastery. He wanted to make known the discovery that had been made, that, through the influence of their friends at court, his release might be formally demanded.

But to this proposal the old man would not listen for one moment. "I know these cunning foxes," he said. "Dost thou think they would ever let him leave those walls alive, after all the denials they have given of his being there? Nay, nay! I should never see him again, and he would never wake to the understanding of things, as he is slowly awakening now. Dost thou know what he asked me today?"

Conrad shook his head. He was wondering whether it would not be better to disobey his grandfather for once, and let their friends know of his discovery. "I would that I could see my father," he said.

"He hath asked about thee; about his little knave, Conrad. 'He is but a weakly babe,' he said to me today; and then for the first time I noticed that he grew restless, as if he wanted to leave his work and go out."

"And he must—oh, he must be rescued from those walls!" said Conrad, glancing across at the monastery opposite.

But the old man shook his head. "Not yet, Conrad, not yet; it would kill him, or send him quite mad, I trow, to bring him into the world again as he is. Nay, nay, trust me; I am waking him up slowly; he doth not comprehend aught of the time that hath passed since he hath been there, or he would not talk of Jerome Faulfisch as a little knave, and thee as a weakly babe; and so, to bring him out into this new world, as it would be to him, where he would not know his own wife or son, would but confuse his weak mind so that it would never grow strong, and he would never know thee, Conrad, for his son—would not believe thou wert his son, but would take some puling infant to his breast and fondle that for thee."

This argument convinced Conrad that his grandfather was right in his present plan of procedure; but still he could not but feel anxious, for suppose the superior should suspect their secret, or stop the work of alteration going on in the monastery!

The old man shuddered at the bare possibility of such a catastrophe; but the next moment he

PULING: *whimpering*

said, laying his hand on Conrad's shoulder, "Thou knowest I was but a Lollard in my love of liberty when I left England; but I wanted help to find my son more than thou or thy friends or the king could give, and I took thy word for it that God would not be offended if I asked Him straight to help me find my boy. Thou knowest the Church hath no prayers for such need as this, and so I could not but ask for myself, and—and, Conrad, I believe He heard the poor old mason without even the saints interfering. It may be—I think it was—something that God alone could help in; and since I began to pray like that it hath been such a comfort and consolation to me. God hath given me such peace and patience and courage to wait, and the superior and all the brethren have such favor toward me, that at last I have found my son; and dost thou think God would show him to me just to snatch him away again? Nay, nay; I trow not. I would not serve my son so; and I trow God, who made man, as thou sayest, in the image of Himself, hath given to fathers a heart somewhat like to His own, in that they will not do aught to hurt them except it be for their good."

Conrad stared in blank amazement at the old man's words. What he said revealed a trust and confidence in God such as he had heard Mistress Margery and one or two others speak of; but he had looked upon these as especially favored—almost saints, according to the Church's ideas; and it never entered his head that ordinary mortals, like himself or his grandfather, could ever attain to such an exalted experience. In point of fact, he had rather looked down upon the honest old mason, for he had often confessed that he could not understand a good deal of what Dr. Wycliffe had written, except that he claimed for all men liberty of soul as well as body; and so, out of his intense love of liberty, he had cast in his lot with his followers and been called a Lollard.

Conrad, however, had gone beyond this. His reason and his intellect had been convinced; he longed to see the Church purified of her abuses and entirely reformed; and that Wycliffe desired more for the individual soul of man than what he had already apprehended as the truth in his teaching, was something rather startling. That there was more—that Wycliffe and Huss and Jerome, with all their clearness of teaching, could only take the soul, and lead it on through clearer light up to a certain point, where God Himself must be met, if there was to be this clear apprehension of God Himself, he was now convinced; but that his grandfather should attain it while he was left far behind was rather puzzling, and somewhat humbling. He had often despised the old man in his heart for not caring more about the intellectual differences between Wycliffe's teaching and that of the Church, and had questioned his right to be called a Lollard, when all he cared about was the liberty it preached. Now it seemed that with this one idea of liberty—the soul's right to approach

APPREHENDED: *understood*

God—he had pushed his way through all the mists and darkness of his old belief that still clung to him, had for himself practically abolished saint and image-worship, and every superstitious fear that could keep him away, and had penetrated into the very presence-chamber of God Himself. He, Ned Trueman, the old mason, who could neither read nor write, and cared little for polemical reasoning except as it exhibited Conrad's learning—who never thought to teach anybody anything, except it might be how to do a little masonwork—he ranked side by side with the world's great teachers, Wycliffe and Huss, and others who had gone before them, who had apprehended and tried to teach the same glorious truths that these now preached with no uncertain sound. Among these stood the humble-minded, honest old workman, while he who aspired to be the next in rank at least to these great ones—he who had labored to master all the learning possible, that he might be called the "seraphic doctor"—was left far behind!

All this was revealed to Conrad as he sat and mused upon what his grandfather had said. It was a very humbling, but a very salutary experience; for, unconsciously, his friends had made so much of him, especially his mother and grandfather, and had made themselves and their individual comfort so entirely subservient to his, that it was not surprising he should think himself of somewhat more importance than he really was.

SALUTARY: *beneficial*

It was well for him, too, perhaps, that his learned friends, Jerome and Master Huss, were away from Prague, and that he heard occasionally how well the work was going on in other parts of Bohemia, now that they were driven from the capital.

The interdict had been removed by the pope since Huss had departed, and the city had resumed its usual bustling appearance, while the altars in the numerous splendid churches blazed again with lights, and priests, robed in "purple and fine linen," with gold-embroidered copes, and miters set with precious stones, swung censers of incense, and gave thanks to God that heresy had been driven from the city; as though Huss were the only heretic, and that which he had so diligently been sowing for years would not yet spring up and bear fruit a hundredfold.

Many of the more prominent friends and adherents of Huss had followed his example, and prudently left the city; for they recalled the time when Janovius and his friends were persecuted to the very death, and they knew that their king was not stronger to protect them against the persecutions of the Church than his father, the Emperor Charles, had been, for both secretly favored these doctrines of the Reformers, although afraid openly to profess them. And so at this time Conrad was left very much to his own reflections, with little to disturb him from the outer world; and he now had time to notice what he had failed to see before—

MITERS: *tall, pointed headdresses worn by the bishops*

the gradual change that had been at work in his mother and grandfather.

His gentle, weak, dependent mother seemed fading away; and yet the worn, grieved look had given place to one of peace and rest, and there was less querulousness in her voice, and fewer complaints were heard about her disappointment at not gaining any tidings of her husband, or her own unhappy life.

Conrad was at a loss to understand this change in her for some time; but one day, when they had been sitting together, Dame Ermengarde suddenly said, "Thy visit to England, Conrad, carried me thither also; and I have been living over again in thought much of the time I spent there. Thou didst not hear the Archbishop Arundel preach the funeral sermon of my mistress, the good Queen Anne; but he spoke some words I have never since forgotten in praise of her diligent study of the Holy Scriptures. She had often enjoined upon us, her attendants, the duty of this study, too; but, as thou knowest, I was ever fearful of offending Holy Church and my mother; and so, although I carefully kept the queen's Book which she gave me, it seemed a fearsome thing to read it, until after I heard the words of Archbishop Arundel; though it hath sometimes been a sore puzzle to me how he could commend my mistress for that which he hath sent others to suffer death by burning for doing—for this reading

QUERULOUSNESS: *grumbling*
ENJOINED UPON US: *directed us*

the Scriptures is now taken as a sign of heresy, I trow."

"Yes, Archbishop Arundel hath forbidden it, and all who do so are accused of heresy, now, in England."

"Then 'tis well I am not in England," said Dame Ermengarde, with a faint smile; "for I would brave being called a heretic even by my mother rather than give up reading God's Word. Conrad, this is, verily, what the queen, my mistress, called it—God's Word; the Word she would have all men and women know in their hearts concerning Him. I have learned to know it, miserable, and weak, and undeserving as I am. He hath taught me what my husband strove to teach me in vain, and what my mistress, also, exhorted me to learn. But I was afraid, Conrad, in those days—afraid of offending the Church, and afraid of dishonoring our family by being called a heretic; but, more than all, afraid of my mother, for—"

"Nay, nay; talk not of my grandam, or I shall grow fierce in my hatred of her for what she hath made my father suffer. Think, my mother; he hath been all these years—"

And then he suddenly stopped, for he was about to betray his grandfather's closely-guarded secret. He could hardly have kept it from his mother a short time before, but he had suddenly acquired a new respect for his grandfather; he was, doubtless, wiser than himself in this, as in some other matters, since this had been the sacred clue that had led him, through a labyrinth of difficulties, straight into the very presence of God.

Dame Ermengarde did not notice Conrad's sudden hesitation, for she herself was deeply moved; but at length she said, "Conrad, if thy father wert with us now, the first lesson he would try to teach thee and me would be to forgive my poor old mother, who was such a blind servant of a blind Church."

"But, my mother, the blindness was willful; she doth not deserve to be forgiven!" replied Conrad.

"Deserve it! And dost thou think any of us ever deserve forgiveness? Nay, nay, it is God's free gift; for what have we ever done but sin against Him? And yet He forgives us not once or twice, but every day. I tell thee, Conrad, no one could deserve His wrath more than thy poor weak mother—no one could deserve His mercy less; but the Lord Jesus died to save the weak and the undeserving, and He died to redeem me. I believe it now—believe the words written in the book: He died 'the just for the unjust.'[1] It cannot be that He can be offered again, as the Church saith He is in the mass, for He bore the sins of the whole world once—carried all the dreadful load that kept us away from God quite out of the way, so that through this sacrifice of Himself for us we may draw near to God, without any merit or good works of our own to make us deserving of His mercy and goodness."

[1] I Peter 3:18

LABYRINTH: *maze*

"And thou hast learned to know this, my mother!" stammered Conrad, at last.

"Thou dost think I have been long in learning it; and, truly, I am but an unprofitable servant, for I had the Book long ere I read it; and when I read it first it was but a wonderful tale to me; I saw not that it was the very Word of God, sent for me."

"Nay, but, Mother, thou hast learned more—" and then, overcome by his emotion, Conrad hastily left the room.

"My grandfather and my mother, too—these whom I had despised as being only half-Lollards—these have passed on before me, and know the hidden truth revealed to Dr. Wycliffe and Master Huss, and which I thought could only be attained by wisdom and learning: while I—I am left far behind! I cannot even pray as doth my mother, 'God be merciful to me a sinner!'[1] for I do not feel as I ought even about this."

Conrad closed the door of his room, and throwing aside his crutches, sank down upon the floor, resting his head upon his folded arms as he leaned against an old chest.

"Will God ever receive me? Can I ever enter His presence, as my grandfather and mother have done? Oh, that I could feel as doth my gentle mother—that I am undeserving of any favor! But I will, I must, be honest; I do not, cannot, feel this. Nay, since I have returned from England I have thought God unkind and unjust, because I could not persuade Mistress Mary to leave her uncle to the care

[1] Luke 18:13

Conrad at Prayer

of Dame Gilpin and come with me to Prague. I have thought I deserved *more* than God hath given me; and so how can I go to Him confessing I am unworthy, when I feel almost as though God were my debtor for doing what I have to help Master Huss here in Bohemia? Can it be that there is no other way of going to God than going empty-handed, as these, my mother and grandfather, have done?—he craving help because he could not help himself, and she praying for mercy simply because the Lord Jesus Christ had died. But, then, what had she to offer that was worthy of God's acceptance? She had refused to listen to my father, or to her mistress, good Queen Anne; but I have applied myself to learn the truth Dr. Wycliffe hath taught; and surely in this there is some merit. It must be some recommendation that a man hath done as I have, and even been called a heretic and Lollard; so surely God hath some favor toward me for these things."

Pride had suggested this latter consideration, and Conrad listened to its voice. Surely there was a way to attain the peace and rest his grandfather and mother enjoyed, less humbling than that by which they had gained it—a royal road for the wise and learned, which he should doubtless discover ere long; and so, trying to dismiss the subject from his thoughts for the present, he went in search of his grandfather, for it was near the time for him to come home from his work at the monastery.

Chapter XX

At Constance

THE Council of Pisa, summoned, in the year 1409, to reform the abuses of the Church, did little beyond ending the schism that had so long rent it into divided factions by deposing both the rival popes and electing another in their stead. He—Alexander—was a man of piety and honesty; but he did not long enjoy the honor that had been conferred upon him; and after his death a successor was chosen who had been a pirate and a murderer, and who still, unrepentant, lived a life of luxury and vice that no monarch in Europe equaled. That there should be another division, another pope declaring himself to be Christ's vicar upon earth, and the pirate pope, John XXIII, to be Antichrist, was inevitable. But now *two* others claimed to be each the true and only successor of St. Peter, in rivalry of John, so that the Church was more divided than ever with this triple claim upon her allegiance.

At length the discontented clamoring of all

RENT: *torn*
VICAR: *representative*
LAITY: *common people*

Christendom for a general council, not only of bishops and cardinals, but one in which the laity could at least be represented by their princes and sovereigns, could no longer be ignored, and a council, general and ecumenical, was at last called to meet in the city of Constance, in the year 1414 A.D. This great council was to be, like the ancient one of Nicæa, an assemblage of the whole Church, or, at least, the Western portion of it, and not to be presided over by the pope—for the claims of the three rival pontiffs were to be submitted to the council; and not only this, but the vital question was to be settled of the supremacy of councils over the pope, or of the pope over councils. Another question was this heresy that had broken out in England and Bohemia. Wycliffe was dead, but his opinions had taken such deep root in the heart of the nation that not even fear of the stake could extirpate them.

There were three notable persons, likewise, to be judged by the council, all bearing the name of John: Pope John XXIII, John Huss, and Jean Petit. The latter had published a book justifying in most plain terms a foul and treacherous murder. In this vindication he had laid down principles subversive of all human society, in direct violation of the commandment of God, and in opposition to the whole religion of Christ.

Proof would be adduced of the sovereign pontiff, John XXIII, being guilty of every known crime—

ECUMENICAL: *including all Christian churches*
SUBVERSIVE OF: *destructive to*
ADDUCED: *brought forward*

crimes at which the heart shudders and revolts; and not only this, but of having made a gain of the profligacy of others, rendering it a source of wealth to himself. John Huss, of irreproachable life, was to be charged with erroneous belief in transubstantiation and the administration of the cup to the laity; and the united wisdom of Europe was to sit in judgment on these three men.

The news that a council had at length been summoned sent a thrill of hope and expectancy through many hearts in every city of Europe. Huss had appealed to a council to judge him; but at the same time neither he nor King Wenzel felt very confident of a favorable verdict; and the Emperor Sigismund, who had summoned the council, was appealed to for a safe-conduct which should guarantee his return to Bohemia after the close of the council.

A nobleman who was strongly attached to him was to go with him; but that Huss himself had some misgivings as to the result of the proceedings, in spite of the promised safe-conduct from the emperor and the protection of his noble patron, was evident from the fact that, just before he left Prague, he sent a letter to a friend, charging him, however, not to open it except in case of his death.

He also wrote a letter to his flock, exhorting them to steadfastness in the truth, and praying for grace that he himself might persevere and not betray the Gospel by cowardice; and he begged

PROFLIGACY: *shameless immorality, reckless extravagance*
BURGHERS: *the inhabitants of a borough or town*

them, also, to pray that he might glorify God by martyrdom, or return to Prague with an unblemished conscience, and with more vigor than ever extirpate the doctrine of Antichrist. Several friends went with him in the train of the knight John de Chlum, and among them our hero, Conrad, who was to act as scribe or secretary either to the nobleman or Master Huss.

They traveled by slow stages, for the fame of Huss had gone before him, and in every town where they stopped friends met him with kindly words either of encouragement or warning. In several towns he held conferences, even with the clergy, parting with them on friendly terms.

At Nuremburg they found the whole city alive with visitors on their way to Constance—bishops and abbots, knights and grave burghers; while artisans and peddlers, following in their wake, crowded every nook and corner where lodgings could be had. Day after day came standards and banners emblazoned with the armorial bearings of princes, of nobles, of knights, of imperial cities, or the silver crozier borne before some bishop or abbot. All the town turned out to gaze at each illustrious visitor, and Master Huss was greeted with hearty cheers as he passed through the crowded streets.

They were met here by the nobleman bearing the imperial safe-conduct, which was couched in the fullest and most explicit terms. John de Chlum, Wenzel de Duba, and Henry de Lazenbach, were charged to keep watch and guard over their

CROZIER: *a staff with a crook or cross on the top*
COUCHED: *worded*

countrymen, who traveled under the special protection of the emperor.

When Conrad read this missive, he dismissed every fear concerning the safety of his beloved master; and when they resumed their journey he gave himself up to the enjoyment of the scene through which they were passing, and of which they formed a part.

Seated on a mule, whose tinkling bells were a fit accompaniment to his thoughts, he could watch the ever-increasing throng of travelers, all journeying in the same direction, through the autumn mists and golden sunshine, until at last, when the gates of Constance itself were reached, it seemed as though some vast central fair was about to be held; for from every converging road that met here came not only trains of ecclesiastics of every order and degree, with princes and ambassadors, but merchants, peddlers, minstrels, and jugglers, from every nation in Europe, with their various attire, habits, and languages.

Constance presented such a spectacle as no other city had ever done since the first general council of the Church, held at Nicæa; and men began to hope that something effectual would at last be done to allay the heart-burnings and schisms, and stop at least some of the numerous slanders that rent the Church.

Pope John had already arrived, and by bribery or flattery was trying to make friends with every

MISSIVE: *message*
ALLAY: *calm*

powerful prince or priest; for he, like John Huss, was to be tried by this council, and he knew the weight of evidence against him. The council was to be opened on the fifth of November, 1415; and by that time there was gathered within its walls all the wisdom of Europe, in the persons of the doctors of canon and civil law, and the representatives of the renowned universities, each of whom would send as their champion their most learned and distinguished professor.

The subjects that were to be considered by the council were already determined; but the order in which they should be brought forward was as yet an open question, and the pope determined to profit by this if possible. The vital question of all—the superiority of the council to the pope, or of the pope to the council—must be postponed; and if postponed, it might be eluded. This would probably be the case, if some matter were taken up in which pope and council were agreed; and what more suitable one could there be than the suppression of heresy? Against this they could unite in almost maddening zeal, and, moreover, for this they had precedents which would go far to establish John as the only lawful pope, and, therefore, amenable to the council only if heresy were proved against him.

The suppression of heresy had been the first care of all councils, from the ancient Nicene to the recent Pisan; indeed, this Council of Constance

AMENABLE: *answerable*

might be taken as a continuation of that of Pisa; and if the Council of Pisa were thus tacitly recognized, Pope John's title, resting, as it did, upon a decree of that council, was irrefragable. So the whole craft of the pope and his Italian cardinals was bent in this direction; for if the pope rendered the signal service of condemning, or of inducing these heretics to recant, surely the council would confirm him in his title against his two rivals.

He knew little about the doctrines of Wycliffe, which Huss was accused of teaching in the university of Prague and the villages of Bohemia; but he knew they were held in detestation by all partisans of the Church; while to the more ignorant they possessed a terror scarcely exceeded, if equaled, by that of witchcraft.

So, quietly, but industriously, the pope set his wits and his followers to work, that this question of which Master Huss was the representative should be the first to occupy the attention of the council. He had no personal ill-will toward the man he had excommunicated—indeed, he received him kindly; for if he could only induce him to recant his heretical opinions, he might become more than a mere pawn in this mighty game of chess that was to be played in the sight of all Europe.

Honest, simple-minded Conrad saw his master not merely acquitted by the council, but triumphantly convincing the whole of that august body of the truth of his doctrines, after this very

TACITLY RECOGNIZED: *accepted by not objecting to it*
IRREFRAGABLE: *indisputable*
SIGNAL: *notable*

favorable reception of himself by the pope; and he wrote a letter to his mother, bidding her tell his grandfather that the long-looked-for, much-talked-of reformation was about to commence—would be inaugurated by this most wonderful and wise Council of Constance, which would shortly accept Master Huss as the teacher and reformer for whom the Church had long been waiting.

These hopes, which in his enthusiasm Conrad viewed as accomplished facts, were cherished by numbers even in Constance; and many friends crowded round Huss; while strangers came, too, in crowds, to hear the man whose name was upon every lip.

John Huss was not the man to shrink in base timidity from avowing here what he had publicly taught in Prague. The Bishop of Constance admonished him, but in vain, and at last forbade his celebrating mass until the ban of excommunication had been formally removed.

But all at once the bright hopes of friends began to dissolve like snow-wreaths from the Alpine slopes. Two of the most bitter foes of Huss, with whom he had been involved in fierce controversy—Palecz and Michael de Causis—came from Prague to accuse him of teaching doctrines not subversive of God's Word, but of the Roman hierarchy. Huss had declared wicked popes, wicked cardinals, wicked prelates, to be utterly without authority, their excommunications void, and their

PARTISANS: *supporters*
AUGUST: *imposing, stately*
INAUGURATED: *begun*

administrations of the sacraments only valid by some nice distinction.

These men had resolved from the first to leave nothing untried that could secure the condemnation of Huss; and so, shortly after their arrival, he was summoned before a consistory of the pope and his cardinals. He obeyed, but at the same time said that he had come to Constance to appear before the council, not a consistory of cardinals. The pope, however, had his own ends to serve, and thought by frequent debates and remands he should at length induce Huss to recant all his errors. How could he, who cared not a pin for religion, understand the stern, unswerving conscientiousness of such a man as Huss? He thought it would be easy to convince him of anything after a few wearying trials, with intermissions of imprisonment, each more strict, as the trials failed to convince him of his folly in persevering so obstinately against the manifest wish of the pope.

And so, four weeks after his arrival in Constance, in utter violation of the terms of his safe-conduct, Huss was imprisoned in the bishop's palace. His friends, in dire alarm, now appealed and protested against this, but all in vain; and soon afterward he was removed, for greater security, to the convent of the black friars. Here he was taken very ill, and was attended by the pope's physician. After his recovery he spent much of his time in writing; and our old friend Conrad was fully employed in copying

CONSISTORY: *assembly*
REMANDS: *sending the prisoner back to wait*
MANIFEST: *clear, obvious*

his works for distribution among his friends. But if Huss was resigned to the Divine will in the matter of his release or condemnation, his friend, de Chlum, was by no means disposed to resign him to the will of his enemies; and, finding that the pope, who had succeeded in leading the council, could not, or would not, order his release, he appealed to the emperor, who had just been crowned at Aix la Chapelle, and was on his way to Constance. Sigismund was very angry, and threatened that the convent doors should be broken open by force, if the pope and cardinals did not release the man who was under his special protection. But his anger and his threats were alike unheeded; and when he reached Constance a short time after, he not only ignored the man he had promised to protect, but was induced to abandon him altogether—to leave him wholly to the mercy of his foes; and what that mercy was likely to be he knew well enough, for Huss was now removed from the Dominican convent to still closer imprisonment.

A missive arrived from Prague, demanding, in strong terms, the liberty of Huss; but the emperor had found that the tide of feeling in the council was too strong against him for any hope of his being able to stem it; and he had staked his fame, his influence, and his popularity on the assembling of this council; and therefore Huss must be sacrificed, if need be, or the council might dissolve without accomplishing anything. Besides, was it

CLOSER: *stricter*

not a doctrine received without question, that no promise, no oath, was binding if made to a heretic? So demands, appeals, expostulations, were alike useless. The council met in solemn conclave, and talked over the crimes of Pope John, and afterward amused themselves with jousts and tournaments, while John Huss lay fettered in a dungeon of the castle of Gotleben.

The pope at length, finding that the emperor had taken the lead of the council out of his hands, and that he was likely to be condemned for his numerous crimes, secretly left the city, and from Schaffhausen sent complaints and hurled defiances at the council, which had asserted itself supreme.

This last act had given renewed hope to Huss and his friends. This was the first step toward the grand reformation that had been so long talked of, so earnestly prayed for. Conrad recalled the talks they had had at Lutterworth of this coming reformation, about which Jerome of Prague and Sir John Oldcastle had felt so confident. It was coming at last! the combined wisdom of Europe would inaugurate the glorious era, and Jerome should be the first to know and rejoice over it; and Conrad wrote thus, begging him to come to Constance and welcome Huss on his release from prison.

EXPOSTULATIONS: *protests*
CONCLAVE: *an assembly of Church officials*

Chapter XXI

Condemnation of Huss

THE news conveyed in Conrad's letter caused the deepest joy among his friends at Prague. From the fact of the council having asserted its authority as superior to that of the pope, they had already drawn the most sanguine conclusions as to the result of Master Huss's trial; and his friend Jerome had already begun to prepare for his departure from Prague. A few, more cautious than the rest, begged him to wait till Huss had been released from prison before venturing to enter Constance; the ardent reformer, however, could brook no delay, but set off as soon as possible on his journey, and entered Constance secretly, as he was protected by no safe-conduct to ensure his return.

Here he found that Conrad and the few friends with him were less sanguine than they had been a short time before.

"Nay, nay; but, now that the council hath asserted its authority as above the pope, wherefore shouldst thou fear?" asked Jerome. "The emperor is—"

ARDENT: *passionate*
BROOK: *stand for, tolerate*

"Talk not of the emperor to me! He gave his imperial word that Master Huss should be protected, and hath he not broken it by suffering him to remain in prison?" exclaimed Conrad.

"But it doth not depend upon the will of the emperor alone. This reform of the Church is anxiously sought by the leaders in the council, by the Cardinals D'Ailly, Gerson, St. Mark, and Zaberella. These are wise and learned men, of purer morals than most of the clergy, and as desirous of seeing their brethren and the Church reformed as Huss himself," replied Jerome, warmly.

"Yes, it is as thou sayest," assented Conrad; "these do desire a reform; but it is not such a reform as Master Huss and Dr. Wycliffe would have. They would purify the lives of the clergy, and have the monks learned instead of ignorant—not that they might teach the people better, but that the Church might be strengthened, and men might no longer be able to deride and point the finger at her for these idle, vicious, ignorant priests. Thinkest thou they would question, far less alter, any established rule of the Church, either in doctrine or ritual? Nay, nay; the reform they are laboring to bring about is for the sake of strengthening the Church against the people. Thou and Master Huss and Dr. Wycliffe would have a reformation for the people, that they may be lifted up into purer, clearer light, and that the corruptions and superstitions of the Church itself should be purified, that they may see this true light."

But Jerome could not resign his fondly cherished dream all at once. He would stay at Constance for a few days at least, and watch the proceedings of the council—hear some of the debates, if possible, and then, if what he saw and heard confirmed the opinion of Conrad, he would leave at once and return to Prague. He soon became convinced that what Conrad had said was only too true, and was preparing to return, when a formal summons was issued by the council for him to appear before them within fourteen days. They offered full freedom of entrance into Constance. His departure must depend upon their judgment of his cause.

But Jerome had already heard enough. He resolved to make good his escape while it was in his power; and he left Constance as secretly as he had entered, and might have reached Prague in safety but for his own impulsiveness. At Hirscham he broke out into some denunciation of the council, and was recognized by some of the clergy as the friend and coadjutor of Huss. He was at once seized and sent prisoner to Constance, thus adding to the anxiety and perplexity of his and Huss' friends.

Huss had been six months in prison when, about the end of May, A.D. 1415, another letter came from Prague, praying the council to hear the cause of their countryman publicly, and deliver him from his noisome dungeon, as it was seriously affecting his health. But a public trial was the last thing they desired. A public recantation of his errors would

NOISOME: *foul-smelling*

have pleased the council, and the emperor too, better than anything else; for, as they had already condemned the doctrine of Wycliffe, they could not but condemn Huss, unless he so recanted; but of this they had but little hope, although they tried every means possible to induce him to do so. He was visited in prison by several of the most learned cardinals, and he was brought up again and again, and his trial protracted day after day, in the hope of wearing out his resistance. More than one form of recantation was drawn up for his signature, but Huss firmly stood by what he had taught in Prague.

Early in July his works and those of Wycliffe were condemned to be publicly burned—all that could be collected in Constance; and this was followed a few days afterward by the condemnation of Huss himself. He was publicly degraded in the cathedral, the last words of this Christian council to him being these: "We devote thy soul to hell;" to which Huss replied: "And I commend my soul to the most merciful Lord Christ Jesus."

He was then led out of the church, two of the executioner's servants walking in front and two behind him. Conrad and several other friends were waiting outside in the street; but when Conrad saw the calm, gentle face of his teacher and friend, all his firmness forsook him. He could not follow with the throng that pressed after the silent cortège to the meadow outside the walls, where a pile of sticks and a post with a rusty chain told all too plainly

PROTRACTED: *drawn out*
DEGRADED: *removed from his position*

what the end of this was to be. No, no; he had seen enough in Constance without that last awful spectacle, for only a short time before he had seen his dear friend Jerome bound to a post and his hands chained to his neck, and in this position he had been ten days; so that what awaited him in the future Conrad knew all too well.

But a sudden thought seized him as he watched the last of the throng pass out of sight. He could do nothing more for Huss—nothing for Jerome here in Constance but what others could do better; he would hasten to Prague, and rouse the citizens to do something to avenge the insult that had been offered to them in this burning of Huss; and it might be that by this means Jerome would be saved from a similar fate.

So while the wreaths of dark smoke ascended from the funereal pile to the cloudless sky, and were reflected in the blue waters of the lovely lake, Conrad was riding with all speed from the city, his heart full of sorrow for his friends, and of vengeance against those who had condemned them; and with this feeling as strong as ever in his heart he reached Prague with the doleful news.

It needed no words of his to arouse the indignation of the citizens. All classes, all conditions of men, rose as if they were moved by one mighty impulse. The king was as angry as the people, and openly denounced the emperor for his treachery, and the council for its barbarous injustice. At a meeting of the magnates of Bohemia an address

CORTÈGE: *procession*
MAGNATES: *political leaders*

was drawn up and signed by sixty nobles, denouncing the execution of Huss; and this was sent without delay to Constance.

The lower classes protested in a different fashion; they rose against the monks and clergy in Prague who had not favored Huss; and no sooner was one riot against the monks quelled than another broke out.

In dire alarm for the safety of himself and the brethren under him, the superior of the Dominican monastery sent for the old mason, to strengthen the walls and gates of the building, lest an attack should be made upon them next. Old Trueman cheerfully obeyed the summons, for he saw in this a possibility of being able to effect his son's escape, when all hope had failed, and every plan that he could devise had been baffled.

By slow and painful stages the lay brother, Sebastian, had been aroused from his waking sleep—his death in life, which he had lived for more than thirty years—and could now recall much of what he had endured when he first entered the monastery. Whether or not he had ever recanted he could not tell, but he knew that several of the brethren had been punished for listening to what he had taught them. Of course, to escape from the monastery was all he desired, when sufficiently aroused to comprehend his situation and the events that had occurred since he had been shut out of the world; and it was well for him, and his father too, that they both knew where to seek for

EFFECT: *accomplish*

strength and patience to wait until this could be securely accomplished before even an attempt was made.

But oh, that weary waiting! The impatient, impetuous old Englishman found that this heart-sickening delay—this hovering between hope and fear—was a trial harder to be borne than any he had yet met with; but, knowing where to seek for grace and strength to bear it, he patiently waited and waited, and hoped for the safe deliverance to come. Trueman had thought—and truly so, for a time—that he was wholly unsuspected; but at last the jealous eyes of one of the older brethren noticed the friendship that had sprung up between the old mason and the half-demented lay brother. No hindrance was offered to this; the two were left to follow their own way; but from that day they were watched, and old Trueman knew it—felt it with a sense that seemed suddenly to have been awakened in him—and from that moment he was ceaselessly on his guard. He also warned his son not to betray anything of the change that had taken place in his mental condition. So wary was old Trueman not to betray anything of his real relationship to the poor drudge, Sebastian, or to make the slightest effort toward releasing him, that at last the superior laughed at the brother who had brought him the news of his suspicions, and the watch was relaxed.

The work on which Trueman was engaged was not completed until some time after Conrad left

Prague for Constance; and with its completion died the old man's last hope of rescuing his son. No opportunity occurred that would give them the least chance of carrying out an escape effectually; and so, after the work was finished inside, hope almost died out of the old man's heart, and he could only pray, with almost the agony of despair, that now he had failed, God would rescue his son by some other means. What this was likely to be he puzzled himself in vain to conceive until the riots against the monks and friars commenced, after the death of Huss. Then hope again awoke in his heart, and he whispered to Conrad that if the infuriated mob would but attack the Dominican monastery, among the rest his father might be rescued, in the confusion of the fight.

Scarcely had the words been spoken when a message was brought to him from the superior, asking him to direct the work of strengthening the walls, in case of an attack. He lost no time in going to the monastery, where he found the panic-stricken brethren in the greatest confusion, from fright and alarm at what had already befallen some of the religious houses of the city.

In the confusion and dismay, he found little difficulty in securing the services of his son, whom he directed to keep close to him. "Thou shalt be free tomorrow, Ned," whispered the old man, as he made a feint of driving in an iron stanchion to secure a window—the very window

FEINT: *show of*

by which he had resolved Ned must escape. He made him understand how this was to be effected. "Thou wilt not have to wait long, I trow, for it will but need a word from thy lad, Conrad, and the mob will be here, instead of frightening the nuns in the next street;" and even while he spoke came the distant, indistinct roar of the approaching crowd. At that sound the old man had taken off part of his own clothes, and put them upon his son, and at the same time covered him with the dust of the brickwork he had been cutting away.

The brethren fled for their lives to the chapel, as they heard the same ominous sound; and when the mob had reached the gates, and had battered a portion of the outer wall down, the old man was preparing to descend from the window, which was only a few feet from the ground.

Young Ned Trueman—no longer Brother Sebastian, since he had gained a footing outside his prison walls—shrunk away in dire alarm, for the noise of sticks and stones, and the blows from the heavy iron bars upon the gate, added to the shouts and groans and yells of, "Down with it! Down with the old crows' nest! Burn it as they burned Master Huss!" made the din almost deafening.

It was well for them, too, that Conrad was one of the first to enter by the breach made in the wall, or they would only have escaped one peril to fall into another; for a mob is not likely to ask questions or wait for explanations when in search of victims to vent their mad wrath upon. But Conrad they did know—they recognized him as the man who had told them where they could most easily make an entrance, and they had some consciousness of hearing him say he wanted to rescue a prisoner; and so the mad yell with which they first greeted the old mason and his son as they saw them was not followed by the death-giving blow or the rough usage, as it probably would have been if Conrad had not been there.

He did not need to be told that the pale, haggard, frightened face he saw before him was that of his father, for he limped forward on his crutches and threw himself into his arms.

"My father, my father!" he gasped, while his father could but feebly clasp Conrad to him; for all this unwonted noise and confusion, after the dread monotony of his life, almost deprived him of his senses again.

The poor old mason's joy was considerably lessened when he saw the effect this scene of terror and confusion had upon his son; and he begged two of the rioters to help them to escape from it as soon as possible, and this the men gladly promised to do, when they understood who they were. He was half-led, half-carried, home, where Dame Ermengarde, scarcely less frightened than the monks themselves, could hardly be persuaded to open the door to them.

"My father, my father!"

"Thou must not tell her yet, Conrad, who our sick friend is," said his grandfather; and Conrad nodded assent, for he was willing to promise anything, now that he had his father at liberty.

Dame Ermengarde was made to comprehend that the sick man would only stay there long enough to put on some of Conrad's clothes in exchange for his own, and take some refreshment, and then they were all to remove at once to the house of a friend at some distance.

Here, in quiet retirement from the din of the city, Ned Trueman once more regained his mental faculties; and then, but not till then, did Dame Ermengarde again see her husband. That they should scarcely recognize each other after the long years of agony through which they had passed is not surprising; but, once knowing each other, years seemed to fall off them, and they seemed to grow young again.

In watching the happiness of his son and daughter old Trueman passed the happiest days of his life; and why Conrad should still be so restless and so dissatisfied he could not understand.

"Yea, as thou sayest, I have my father now," replied Conrad; "but I have lost the hope of my life; there will never be a reformation now, since this Council of Constance hath burned Jerome as they did Huss;" and Conrad could say no more.

FACULTIES: *abilities*

Chapter XXII

Conclusion

EIGHTEEN years have passed since we last chronicled any event affecting the personages of our story—eighteen years of battle and bloodshed, of riots and massacres, at the relation of which the blood runs cold.

Now once more the Bohemians—the representatives of those who hold the opinions of Huss—appear before a general council of the Church, which assembled at Basle, A.D. 1431-1433.

Among the attendants on this august body are our old friend Conrad, with Peter Payne, an Englishman, and the warrior-priest Procopius, who had led the Hussite troops from victory to victory, and Roçana, a theologian of great eloquence and learning. The three latter are the accredited Bohemian ambassadors to the council—not this time to be tried and condemned, as were Huss and Jerome by the Council of Constance. No, no; the Council of Basle was not likely to repeat the mistake made by that body, for the emperor knew now to his cost what a province in revolt meant, and Bohemia had achieved such splendid victories under her generals, Zisca and Procopius, that Germany was now in alarm for her own safety, and the council was ready to tolerate the heresy of the insurgents for the sake of peace. But in the midst of this present security Conrad often recalled the time when, at Constance, he had sought to hide in obscure hostelries, never staying long in one neighborhood, lest he should become known as a friend of Huss.

He was talking of this one day to his friends, and of that time when he first met Jerome at the hostelry in Lutterworth. "Two," said he, "Sir John Oldcastle and Jerome Faulfisch—have died; been burned for the reformation they never saw. I would that they were here this day, to see our reformation triumphant;" and then, as the thought of other friends in England who now lay languishing in prison for this same cause recurred to him, his thoughts grew almost too painful for utterance, and he turned aside to hide the emotion he could not but feel.

At length Conrad resumed the conversation with his friends. "Our cause is triumphant now," he said; "be wary lest ye betray anything for which the blood of Bohemians has been spilled like water."

"But the council hath promised to concede all we ask—the communion in both kinds," said Roçana.

"But that is not *all!*" burst forth Procopius and Conrad, in a breath. "We demand our rights, as set forth in the four articles of Prague: freedom to be taught by our ministers throughout the realm; for communion in both kinds; that the clergy shall not hold estates nor mingle in secular affairs; that deadly sins shall be punished by the magistrate, and that no indulgences shall be sold for money. These were the articles that *must* be adhered to!" Conrad said.

But Roçana shook his head. "The council will not concede as much," he said.

"The council shall concede more! the articles of Prague are not enough!" exclaimed Procopius.

Payne sided with Procopius, other friends with Roçana; and so the strife went on among themselves. The council, which would far rather have treated these leaders of the Hussites as they had Huss himself than grant any concession at all, was not slow to take advantage of these divisions, dragging out their deliberations to an interminable length.

The council had other affairs on hand besides this of these Bohemian heretics. Like its predecessor, it had been mainly convoked to amend the morals of the clergy; and the question of marriage was once more propounded, and by some most earnestly advocated. They were now in communication with the Emperor of the East and the Patriarch of Constantinople; for Western help to drive back the all-conquering Turks was urgently needed; and the price demanded was the reconciliation of the Greek or Eastern Church. Now

INTERMINABLE: *endless*
CONVOKED: *called together*

these admitted marriage among their priests, and so it would be a fitting time to admit it here; and if this were sanctioned by the council there was little doubt but that it would be eagerly accepted by the main body of the clergy; and this would re-establish the principle set forth by the Council of Constance—the superiority of council over pope. This question was agitating not only the Church, but the whole of Europe now, for Pope Eugenius had summoned a rival council in Italy, under his own presidency, disdaining that of Basle, presided over by the emperor. So there were anathemas and denunciations to be hurled at each other by these two infallible councils, besides the weightier business of outbidding each other for the attendance of the Greek patriarch and bishops at their respective councils.

But while the Bohemians were kept waiting in Basle, quarreling among themselves, the Greeks came to Italy; and a hollow adjustment of the differences in creed was entered into with the pope's council; while that of Basle decided that the celibacy of the clergy must still continue an abiding law of the Church.

The Bohemians, divided among themselves, were easily managed by the council. The communion in both kinds, upon which all were agreed, was conceded. The four articles of Prague were either eluded or compromised, and the ambassadors returned home—to lay down the sword, indeed, but to begin, or rather to continue, a polemical strife

PROPOUNDED: *presented for discussion or consideration*
ADMITTED: *permitted*

that ended at last in the true followers of Huss being driven to seek refuge in the woods and forests, where they made common cause with a detachment of the persecuted Waldensians, living in caves and suffering innumerable privations for they dared not light a fire by day or appear in a town or village except by stealth: and thus ended, or, rather died, the Sclavonic Reformation—the reformation inaugurated by the sword, and once promising such splendid success.

Was it wonderful that Conrad, baffled, disappointed, and never yet having found that rest and peace for his soul that he so ardently longed for, should become at last a soured, embittered old man? But so it was; the years had slipped away again, and even the Council of Basle was little more than a memory to him—a something that he talked of bitterly and angrily to his aged mother and father, as having ended what the Council of Constance had so unwittingly begun—the Bohemian Reformation.

Dame Ermengarde and her husband had glided into a calm, happy old age, after the stormy, sorrowful years of their early wedded life. Together they had watched and waited upon their father, to whom, under God, they owed their reunion, until the final call came, and old Ned Trueman was summoned to an inheritance better than any land tenure that could be devised—the "inheritance of the saints in light,"[1] "the building of God... eternal in the heavens," where neither wisdom,

[1] COLOSSIANS 1:12
WONDERFUL: *surprising*

nor learning, nor wealth, nor power, is needful to establish a claim, but faith in the Lord Jesus Christ only.

Conrad was not in Bohemia when his grandfather died, but the old man's last words were for him "the little knave who would be a seraphic doctor." Dame Ermengarde wished he could have seen the peaceful end of the sturdy old English mason, who, in the midst of all his longings to go back to his native land before he died, could yet say the Lord's prayer from his heart, "Thy will be done."[1]

After the close of the Hussite war, and that delusive peace concluded with the Council of Basle, Conrad wandered about through the countries of Europe, returning now and again to his home in Tábor—the stronghold built by the Hussites outside the city of Prague, and where often in the midst of the wildest alarms and preparations for war Dame Ermengarde had lived in undisturbed peace.

But he had never remained long with them before the old restlessness would return. He would relate all he knew of the strange things and people he had met with in his travels; and when the wonder or the novelty of relating these had gone he would depart again, often to the great grief of his mother and father.

Once when he came home he related how he had met with a man who told him that books would no longer need to be written, and he had showed him some blocks of wood upon which letters were

[1] MATTHEW 6:10
DELUSIVE: *false*

cut, that, being inked, could be pressed upon the parchment again and again. His master, one John Geinsfleish, of Haerlem, had been amusing himself one day by cutting letters on a tree, and from this Master Coster had got his idea of cutting them in blocks of wood.

Of course, Conrad ridiculed the idea of anything displacing the use of the pen in the multiplication of books; but when, after a lengthened tour, he returned from Paris about the year 1452, he brought with him a parcel about which he seemed in great perplexity. He had brought it from Paris, where he had bought it of Master John Faustus, who had shortly afterward been accused of witchcraft and thrown into prison. He told his mother this as he lifted the heavy, cumbersome parcel with some difficulty onto the table.

Gentle Dame Ermengarde, as timid as ever, started at the word "witchcraft," and would have run out of the house, if Conrad had not assured her that the parcel contained nothing but what was good—what she had often handled before, and what her beloved mistress, good Queen Anne, prized above all her treasures. But the old lady still shook her head doubtfully when she looked on the strange black letters she could not read.

"Be not affrighted, my mother; it is the Bible—all the Bible in these two books; and 'tis made by the new invention called printing. Dost thou remember, I told thee of the strange wooden letters Master Coster showed me? He showed them to others besides, and Master Faustus thought if they could be made in metal instead of being cut in wood it must be better, and so he hath done it, and can make more Bibles in a month with his printing-press than I could write in two years."

The Printing Press

This last announcement only frightened his mother more; but his father tottered forward, and without any fear laid his hand upon the book.

"I am too old to see to read this Bible. But if, as thou sayest, it is of truth the Word of God, and can be made so fast and so cheap that many, and not few, can possess it, then—then there is hope of a reformation yet!"

The old man spoke with fire and energy, and almost forgot to lean upon his stick as he passed his hand lovingly and tenderly across the sacred page, that was to his dimmed eyes but a blurred sheet of parchment.

Conrad's eyes flashed for a moment with something of their old light, but he shook his head mournfully the next minute. "Nay, nay, that hope hath died now; seek not to raise it again," he said. "I am content to let it go now, for I have learned that God hath His hidden ones even among the monks of the corrupt Roman Church. I will tell thee of this anon; but speak not again to me of a reformation since the sword of Bohemia hath failed!"

"Ah, the sword of Bohemia hath failed!" said his father, with a deep-drawn sigh; "but didst thou never hear, my Conrad, of 'the sword of the Spirit, which is the Word of God?'[1] If this be unsheathed, if this be sent out into all the land, there will, there must, be light at last—light brighter than Masters Wycliffe or Huss ever saw—light compared with which ours is but as the first streak of day-dawn to the noontide sun."

"It may be—God grant it may be—as thou sayest! And I wish Master Faustus Godspeed in his work, and that he may be speedily released from prison; but speak not again of a reformation to me."

Finding the subject was painful to his son, the old man desisted; but, if he had not known that

[1] Ephesians 6:17

this hope of his son's life had at last been utterly given up, he would certainly have thought that he had taken hold of it again. That a great change had taken place in Conrad no one could doubt; but it was some time before anyone could account for it, and then only to his mother did he impart the secret of which he had at last become possessed.

"My mother, I have learned it at last—learned the secret you and my dear old grandfather learned so long ago; I have found my way to God Himself. I thought to learn it by study and philosophy, by wisdom and learning, by teaching the new and better way taught by Wycliffe and Huss; but God hath confounded all my wisdom, and it was at last by the teaching of a black friar that I saw my way out of the darkness of sin into the light of God's truth."

"A black friar! a Dominican monk! one of those who persecuted thy father almost unto death!" exclaimed his mother.

"Ah, 'tis even as thou sayest. I was in France, and met with a Spanish monk, one Vincent Ferrer. As thou knowest, I rarely consort with monks; but this one was preaching in a narrow road, and by reason of the crowd my mule could not pass, and I heard there words such as Master Huss himself might have taught—words that were suited to me as though the monk had known my hidden life. I went and spoke to him afterward, and he said I should have a book he had written, one I would like to read—a book on spiritual life. Listen, my mother, for this is written from the monk's book: 'Dost thou desire to study to advantage? Consult God more than books, and ask Him humbly to make thee understand what thou readest. Go from time to time to be refreshed at the feet of Christ, under His cross. Some moments of repose there give fresh vigor and new light: interrupt thy study by short but fervent supplications.' My mother, if I could but have learned that fifty years ago—gained the peace these words have brought me when I first came back to Bohemia—my life would have been different, I trow. I should not have urged our citizens of Prague to take up the sword to win a reformation by bloodshed; for how can peace—'the peace of God, which passeth all understanding'[1]—be gained by earthly weapons? So I have laid down the hope at last, the dearest hope of my life—dearer even than Mistress Mary Winchester, whose pure, sweet life was worn out in a noisome prison for this same hope, and now waits in heaven for me, and for the hope she died for to be fulfilled. It may be we shall see it together there; but not here, not in this world."

Conrad had thought this hope not only dead, but buried; but it was wakened again to a transient life a few months afterward. He had just closed his mother's eyes in death, and was expecting to lay his father in the tomb with her, when he was asked to go to Constantinople with some other Hussite leaders, to form an alliance with the Greek Church.

[1] PHILIPPIANS 4:7

REPOSE: *rest*

TRANSIENT: *brief*

He had taken so little part in public affairs lately, devoting himself so exclusively to the care of his aged mother and father, who were both fast tottering to the grave under their weight of fourscore years, that he had heard nothing of the reunion of the different sects into which the Hussites had been broken up, or that Roçana, still anxious for a reformation, had at last prevailed upon the States of the kingdom to solicit a reunion with the Greek Church.

A so-called union had been entered into with the pope and the Council of Florence when the Council of Basle was sitting; but it had been repudiated with scorn by the people when their bishops returned, and now they hated with greater intensity the Church of Rome.

All this was explained to Conrad by the messengers of Archbishop Roçana, but he gravely shook his head, saying: "The Greeks may, as thou sayest, hate the Romans, and hatred may bind two peoples together for a little while; but love only can make them keep together. The archbishop would, doubtless, be glad to see a reformation, being urged thereto by his people; but a reformation with hatred for its basis will never be God's reformation, I trow."

But when his father died, a few weeks afterward, and was laid in the grave beside his mother, Conrad began to think more about the archbishop's plan of an alliance with the Greek Church; and at

REPUDIATED: *rejected*

last he was so far prevailed upon as to consent to accompany the messengers to Constantinople.

But, alas, for human hopes! just as the preparations for his journey were complete came the direful news of the sacking of Constantinople by the Turks, and the final overthrow of the Greek empire. Europe stood horror-stricken at the news, for whither would the all-conquering Turks next march? It was the deathblow to Conrad's faintly reviving hope, and it was laid at rest forever.

Could anyone have told him that these relentless Mohammedan victors who had driven Christianity out of Constantinople, and Pope Nicholas V, with his love of books and learning and hatred of all heresy, were to be the main instruments in God's hands for bringing about that for which he had hoped so long, he would have said it was impossible. But He who uses the most unlikely means to accomplish His purposes was slowly but surely gathering together the materials and workers that were to bring about that for which the nations, as well as individuals, had sighed in vain.

Conrad heard of the flight of many of the scholars and philosophers from Constantinople to Rome, whither they had been drawn by the pope's love of learning and the encouragement he gave to all scholars. He heard, too, of the release of Faustus from prison, and a further improvement being made in the art of printing; and, though he sometimes recalled his aged father's words about this "sword of the Spirit," how could he know that this 'little cloud'[1] no bigger than a man's hand, was yet the cloud destined to break in showers of blessing on all lands?

No, Conrad could not hope any longer, but he could pray; and among his friends—the United Brethren, whom he joined on the confines of Moravia—none prayed more earnestly, more fervently, more constantly, than Conrad; but he saw not that for which he prayed—THE REFORMATION.

The End

[1] I KINGS 18:44

ON THE CONFINES: *in the region*

ABOUT THE AUTHOR

Emma Leslie (1837-1909), whose actual name was Emma Dixon, lived in Lewisham, Kent, in the south of England. She was a prolific Victorian children's author who wrote over 100 books. Emma Leslie's first book, *The Two Orphans,* was published in 1863 and her books remained in print for years after her death. She is buried at the St. Mary's Parish Church, in Pwllcrochan, Pembroke, South Wales.

Emma Leslie brought a strong Christian emphasis into her writing and many of her books were published by the Religious Tract Society. Her extensive historical fiction works covered many important periods in church history. Her writing also included a short booklet on the life of Queen Victoria published in the 50th year of the Queen's reign.

Emma Leslie Church History Series

GLAUCIA THE GREEK SLAVE

A Tale of Athens in the First Century

After the death of her father, Glaucia is sold to a wealthy Roman family to pay his debts. She tries hard to adjust to her new life but longs to find a God who can love even a slave. Meanwhile, her brother, Laon, struggles to find her and to earn enough money to buy her freedom. But what is the mystery that surrounds their mother's disappearance years earlier and will they ever be able to read the message in the parchments she left for them?

THE CAPTIVES

Or, Escape from the Druid Council

The Druid priests are as cold and cruel as the forest spirits they claim to represent, and Guntra, the chief of her tribe of Britons, must make a desperate deal with them to protect those she loves. Unaware of Guntra's struggles, Jugurtha, her son, longs to drive the hated Roman conquerors from the land. When he encounters the Christian centurion, Marcinius, Jugurtha mocks the idea of a God of love and kindness, but there comes a day when he is in need of love and kindness for himself and his beloved little sister. Will he allow Marcinius to help him? And will the gospel of Jesus Christ ever penetrate the brutal religion of the proud Britons?

Emma Leslie Church History Series

OUT OF THE MOUTH OF THE LION

Or, The Church in the Catacombs

When Flaminius, a high Roman official, takes his wife, Flavia, to the Colosseum to see Christians thrown to the lions, he has no idea the effect it will have. Flavia cannot forget the faith of the martyrs, and finally, to protect her from complete disgrace or even danger, Flaminius requests a transfer to a more remote government post. As he and his family travel to the seven cities of Asia Minor mentioned in Revelation, he sees the various responses of the churches to persecution. His attitude toward the despised Christians begins to change, but does he dare forsake the gods of Rome and embrace the Lord Jesus Christ?

SOWING BESIDE ALL WATERS

A Tale of the World in the Church

There is newfound freedom from persecution for Christians under the emperor, Constantine, but newfound troubles as well. Errors and pagan ways are creeping into the Church, while many of the most devoted Christians are withdrawing from the world into the desert as hermits and nuns. Quadratus, one of the emperor's special guards, is concerned over these developments, even in his own family. Then a riot sweeps through the city and Quadratus' home is ransacked. When he regains consciousness, he finds that his sister, Placidia, is gone. Where is she? And can the Church handle the new freedom, and remain faithful?

Emma Leslie Church History Series

FROM BONDAGE TO FREEDOM

A Tale of the Times of Mohammed

At a Syrian market two Christian women are sold as slaves. One of the slaves ends up in Rome where Bishop Gregory is teaching his new doctrine of "purgatory" and the need for Christians to finish paying for their own sins. The other slave travels with her new master, Mohammed, back to Arabia, where Mohammed eventually declares himself to be the prophet of God. In Rome and Arabia, the two women and countless others fall into the bondage of man-made religions—will they learn at last to find true freedom in the Lord Jesus Christ alone?

THE MARTYR'S VICTORY

A Story of Danish England

Knowing full well they may die in the attempt, a small band of monks sets out to convert the savage Danes who have laid waste to the surrounding countryside year after year. The monks' faith is sorely tested as they face opposition from the angry Priest of Odin as well as doubts, sickness and starvation, but their leader, Osric, is unwavering in his attempts to share the "White Christ" with those who reject Him. Then the monks discover a young Christian woman who has escaped being sacrificed to the Danish gods—can she help reach those who had enslaved her and tried to kill her?

GYTHA'S MESSAGE

A Tale of Saxon England

Having discovered God's love for her, Gytha, a young slave, longs to escape the violence and cruelty of the world and devote herself to learning more about this God of love. Instead she lives in a Saxon household that despises the name of Christ. Her simple faith and devoted service bring hope and purpose to those around her, especially during the dark days when England is defeated by William the Conqueror. Through all of her trials, can Gytha learn to trust that God often has greater work for us to do *in* the world than *out* of it?

Emma Leslie Church History Series

LEOFWINE THE MONK
Or, The Curse of the Ericsons
A Story of a Saxon Family

Leofwine, unlike his wild, younger brother, finds no pleasure in terrorizing the countrside, and longs to enter a monastery. Shortly after he does, however, he hears strange rumors of a monk who preaches "heresy". Unable to stop thinking about these new ideas, Leofwine at last determines to leave the monastery and England. Leofwine's search for inner peace takes him to France and Rome and finally to Jerusalem, but in his travels, he uncovers a plot against his beloved country. Will he be able to help save England? And will he ever find true rest for his troubled soul?

ELFREDA THE SAXON
Or, The Orphan of Jerusalem
A Sequel to Leofwine

When Jerusalem is captured by the Muslims, Elfreda, a young orphan, is sent back to England to her mother's sister. Her aunt is not at all pleased to see her, and her uncle fears she may have brought the family curse back to England. Elfreda's cousin, Guy, who is joining King Richard's Crusade, promises Elfreda that he will win such honor as a crusader that the curse will be removed. Over the years that follow, however, severe trials befall the family and Guy and Elfreda despair of the curse ever being lifted. Is it possible that there is One with power stronger than any curse?

DEARER THAN LIFE
A Story of the Times of Wycliffe

When a neighboring monastery lays claim to one of his fields, Sir Hugh Middleton refuses to yield his property, and further offends the monastery by sending his younger son, Stephen, to study under Dr. John Wycliffe. At the same time, Sir Hugh sends his elder son, Harry, to serve as an attendant to the powerful Duke of Lancaster. As Wycliffe seeks to share the Word of God with the common people, Stephen and Harry and their sisters help spread the truth, but what will it cost them in the dangerous day in which they live?

www.SalemRidgePress.com

EMMA LESLIE CHURCH HISTORY SERIES

BEFORE THE DAWN

A Tale of Wycliffe and Huss

To please her crippled grandson, Conrad, Dame Ursula allows a kindly blacksmith and his friend, Ned Trueman, to visit the boy. Soon, however, she becomes suspicious that the men belong to the despised group who are followers of Dr. John Wycliffe, and she passionately warns Conrad of the dangers of evil "heresy". He decides to become a famous teacher in the Church so he can combat heresy, but he wonders why all the remedies of the Church fail to cure him. And why do his mother and grandmother refuse to speak of the father he has never known?

FAITHFUL, BUT NOT FAMOUS

A Tale of the French Reformation

Young Claude Leclerc travels to Paris to begin his training for the priesthood, but he is not sure *what* he believes about God. One day he learns the words to an old hymn and is drawn to the lines about "David's Royal Fountain" that will "purge every sin away." Claude yearns to find this fountain, and at last dares to ask the famous Dr. Lefèvre where he can find it. His question leads Dr. Lefèvre to set aside his study of the saints and study the Scriptures in earnest. As Dr. Lefèvre grasps the wonderful truth of salvation by grace, he wants to share it with Claude, but Claude has mysteriously disappeared. Where is he? And is France truly ready to receive the good news of the gospel of Jesus Christ?

Church History for Younger Readers

SOLDIER FRITZ

A Story of the Reformation

by Emma Leslie

Illustrated by C. A. Ferrier

Young Fritz wants to follow in the footsteps of Martin Luther and be a soldier for the Lord, so he chooses a Bible from the peddler's pack as his birthday gift. When his father, the Count, goes off to war, however, Fritz and his mother and little sister are forced to flee into the forest to escape being thrown in prison for their new faith. Disguising themselves as commoners, they must trust the Lord as they wait and hope for the Count to rescue them. But how will he ever be able to find them?

Additional Titles Available From

Salem Ridge Press

DOWN THE SNOW STAIRS

Or, From Goodnight to Goodmorning

by Alice Corkran

Illustrated by Gordon Browne R. I.

On Christmas Eve, eight-year-old Kitty cannot sleep, knowing that her beloved little brother is critically ill due to her own disobedience. Traveling in a dream to Naughty Children Land, she meets many strange people, including Daddy Coax and Lady Love. Kitty longs to return to the Path of Obedience but can she resist the many temptations she faces? Will she find her way home in time for Christmas? An imaginative and delightful read-aloud for the whole family!

YOUNG ROBIN HOOD

by George Manville Fenn

Illustrated by Victor Venner

In the days of Robin Hood, a young boy named Robin is journeying through Sherwood Forest when suddenly the company is surrounded by men in green. Deserted in the commotion by an unfaithful servant, Robin finds himself alone in the forest. After a miserable night, Robin is found by Little John. Robin is treated kindly by Robin Hood, Maid Marian and the Merry Men, but how long must he wait for his father, the Sheriff of Nottingham, to come to take him home?

www.SalemRidgePress.com

Fiction for Younger Readers

MARY JANE – HER BOOK
by Clara Ingram Judson
Illustrated by Francis White

This story, the first book in the Mary Jane series, recounts the happy, wholesome adventures of five-year-old Mary Jane and her family as she helps her mother around the house, goes on a picnic with the big girls, plants a garden with her father, learns to sew and more!

MARY JANE – HER VISIT
by Clara Ingram Judson
Illustrated by Francis White

In this story, the second book in the Mary Jane series, five-year-old Mary Jane has more happy, wholesome adventures, this time at her great-grandparents' farm in the country where she hunts for eggs, picks berries, finds baby rabbits, goes to the circus and more!

Historical Fiction for Younger Readers

AMERICAN TWINS OF THE REVOLUTION

by Lucy Fitch Perkins

General Washington has no money to pay his discouraged troops and twins Sally and Roger are asked by their father, General Priestly, to help hide a shipment of gold which will be used to pay the American soldiers. Unfortunately, British spies have also learned about the gold and will stop at nothing to prevent it from reaching General Washington. Based on a true story, this is a thrilling episode from our nation's history!

MARIE'S HOME

Or, A Glimpse of the Past

by Caroline Austin

Illustrated by Gordon Browne R. I.

Eleven-year-old Marie Hamilton and her family travel to France at the invitation of Louis XVI, just before the start of the French Revolution. There they encounter the tremendous disparity between the proud French Nobility and the oppressed and starving French people. When an enraged mob storms the palace of Versailles, Marie and her family are rescued from grave danger by a strange twist of events, but Marie's story of courage, self-sacrifice and true nobility is not yet over! Honor, duty, compassion and forgiveness are all portrayed in this uplifting story.

Historical Fiction by William W. Canfield

THE WHITE SENECA

Illustrated by G. A. Harker

Captured by the Senecas, fifteen-year-old Henry Cochrane grows to love the Indian ways and becomes Dundiswa—the White Seneca. When Henry is captured by an enemy tribe, however, he must make a desperate attempt to escape from them and rescue fellow captive, Constance Leonard. He will need all the skills he has learned from the Indians, as well as great courage and determination, if he is to succeed. But what will happen to the young woman if they do reach safety? And will he ever be able to return to his own people?

AT SENECA CASTLE

Illustrated by G. A. Harker

In this sequel to *The White Seneca*, Henry Cochrane, now eighteen, faces many perils as he serves as a scout for the Continental Army. General Washington is determined to do whatever it takes to stop the constant Indian attacks on the settlers and yet Henry is torn between his love for the Senecas and his loyalty to his own people. As the Army advances across New York State, Henry receives permission to travel ahead and warn his Indian friends of the coming destruction. But will he reach them in time? And what has happened to the beautiful Constance Leonard whom he had been forced to leave in captivity a year earlier?

THE SIGN ABOVE THE DOOR

Young Prince Martiesen is ruler of the land of Goshen in Egypt, where the Hebrews live. Eight plagues have already come upon Egypt and now Martiesen has been forced by Pharaoh to further increase the burden of the Hebrews. Martiesen, however, is in love with the beautiful Hebrew maiden, Elisheba, whom he is forbidden by Egyptian law to marry. As the nation despairs, the other nobles turn to Martiesen for leadership, but before he can decide what to do, Elisheba is kidnapped by the evil Peshala and terrifying darkness falls over the land. An exciting tale woven around the events of the Exodus from the Egyptian perspective!

Adventure by George Manville Fenn

YUSSUF THE GUIDE

Being the Strange Story of the Travels in Asia Minor of Burne the Lawyer, Preston the Professor, and Lawrence the Sick

Illustrated by John Schönberg

Young Lawrence, an invalid, convinces his guardians, Preston the Professor and Burne the Lawyer, to take him along on an archaeological expedition to Turkey. Before they set out, they engage Yussuf as their guide. Through the months that follow, the friends travel deeper and deeper into the remote regions of central Turkey on their trusty horses in search of ancient ruins. Yussuf proves his worth time and time again as they face dangers from a murderous ship captain, poisonous snakes, sheer precipices, bands of robbers and more. Memorable characters, humor and adventure abound in this exciting story!

CPSIA information can be obtained at www.ICGtesting.com
Printed in the USA
LVOW070737240313

325713LV00001B/10/P